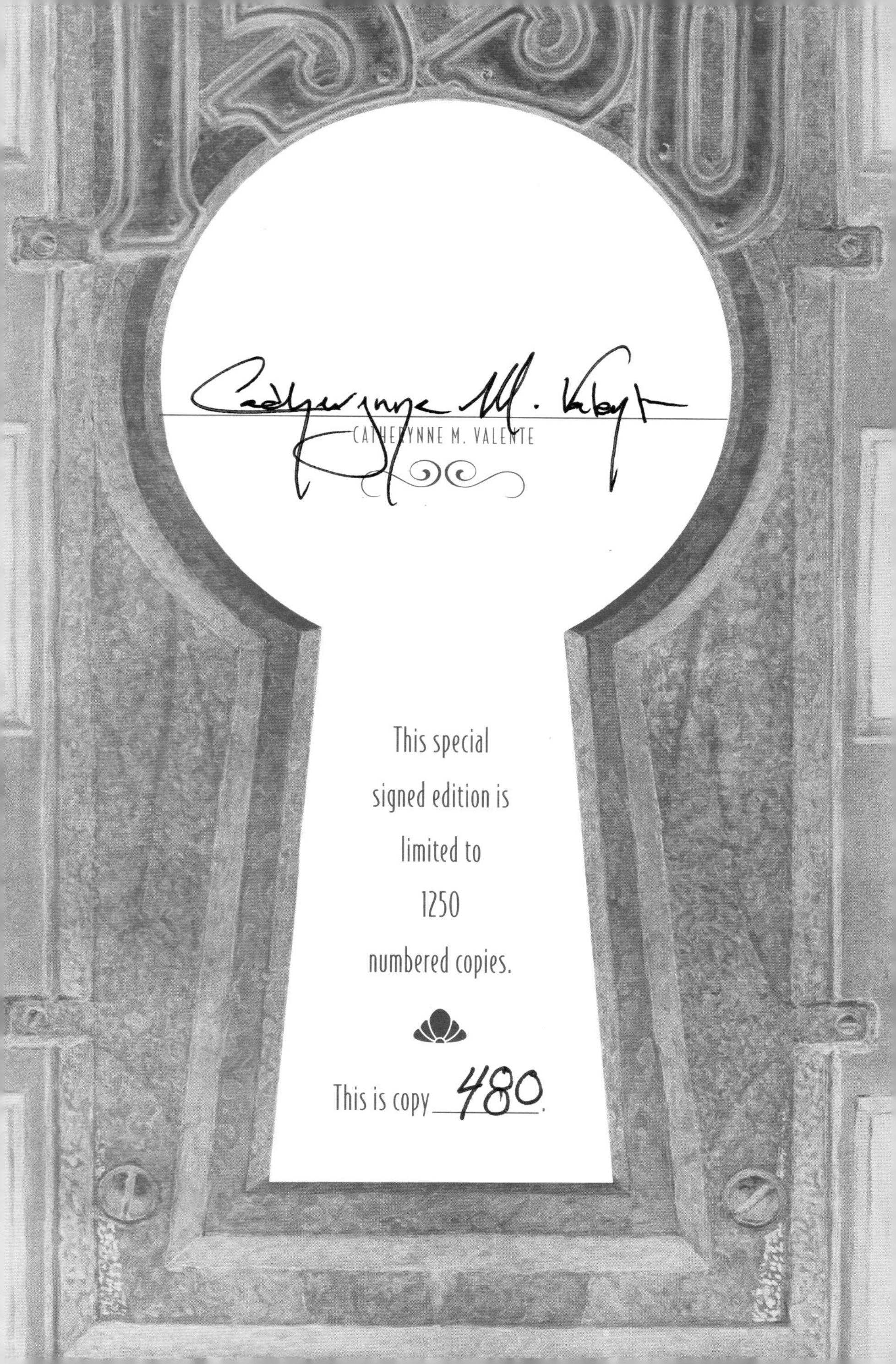
CATHERYNNE M. VALENTE
This special
signed edition is
limited to
1250
numbered copies.
This is copy 480.

SPEAK EASY

SPEAK EASY

CATHERYNNE M. VALENTE

SUBTERRANEAN PRESS 2015

First Edition

ISBN
978-1-59606-727-1

Subterranean Press
PO Box 190106
Burton, MI 48519

subterraneanpress.com

For Helen, who introduced
me to a certain building

For Heath, who speaks more
easily than anyone I know

And for those wild departed
souls who danced awhile
and then no more

Part I: PANTHER SWEAT

CHECK-IN

THERE'S THIS RAGAMUFFIN CITY out east, you follow? Sitting pretty with a river on each arm, lit up in her gladdest rags since 1624. She'll tell you she's seen it all, boy howdy, the deep down and the high up, champagne and syphilis, pearls and puke. Oh, she's a cynical doll, nothing new to her.

Don't you believe it.

Treat her right and she'll open up to you, as innocent as Eden and twice as naked. She's got secrets, sure, who doesn't? Pour me a snort and I'll spill, mister. Spot me a meal and I'll show you the goods.

If you go looking for it, just about halfway uptown and half-way downtown, there's this hotel stuck like a pin all the way through the world. Up on the roof of the Artemisia it's heaven in a handbag, green grass and golden chickens laying golden eggs under the telephonigraph wires, five hundred if there's one. They got Chinese ducks the color of nose-powder, twelve she-goats descended straight down from the girl who gave her tit to a Titan, a coupla Jersey cows giving milk as sweet as maple syrup, bees like gold buttons closing up the clouds, sheep just busting out fleece that spins better than silk. Ever got drunk on a tomato? Hopped up on cucumbers? Well, then you never ate outta the garden on top of the Artemisia. And I swear, up there in the sky? They got a little black bear as tame as a kitten. I hear tell he goes by Rutherford and learned himself to growl "I love you." That's how you know it's heaven: the goats don't eat the sugar peas and the ducks don't fly off and even the fella with the claws knows about love.

Down inside the Artemisia it's this mortal coil all over. Earthly delights on every floor. Says hotel on the neon but most folks live there on the permanent, or as permanent as anything could be in a city that'd eat itself just to grow another block. Showgirls on nine, jazzmen on four, starlets, molls, and debs on seven, abortionists and poisoners and bankers all shufflin' together on three and the real heavy sugar up high: baseball players and bootleggers and bought cops who never busted a joint-a-vous since the Amendment. All the doors stand double-wide to wedge in pianos, card tables, bathtub stills. Real bodhisattvas and down-dirty despots bouncin' and shakin' those red halls: Russian composers on rolly-skates, outfielders tootin' saxophones, tenors practicing archery on big buck glass-eyed deer heads, writers shimmying in bare feet. Poor lambs, but the rent and the drink, they do come before the shine and the shoes. Some damned body rolled out a golf course in the east ballroom, flattened out that green with an iron like it was Pan's own shirtfront. Ain't nothing out there in the city some fool didn't drag in through the service entrance. Everybody said one of these days the moon'd come rolling in like a dining table, COD. Up on her side, boys! Mind the chandeliers!

You never saw girls like those glitter janes with their sequin crowns. You never saw boys like those velvet fellas getting their edge, neither. If Eve went door to door with her apple, not a soul in the Artemisia wouldn't have grabbed it, planted a kiss on old Mama Fig Leaf, and had that shiny red temptation turned into the applejack of good and evil within an hour.

And down below? Oh, baby, it's dark down there in the underworld. Barrels of strike-me-dead skee rolling in full and out empty, stills working full-time, trickling out aqua mortis like the fountain of youth meant to call in all her debts at once. Every hour some long black Duisenberg slows up right into the basement, full of Canadian busthead, Mexican tea, or girls like a matched set of earrings. Down there in the shadows the dandies got themselves a swimming pool like a lake of tears, decked out with silver lanterns on every wall and red silk cabanas full of bath-house boys, svelte sibyls in pomade and not a whole lot else. Those kids'll have you opium or coke on a gold plate before you know you want it. Come midnight that pool's gonna look like a Bosch painting, you follow? The water'll fizz black with running mascara. Fifteen minutes in the basement is a lifetime up above. And the closer you get to the basement the more you get confused on the matters of swell and dastard. Just one little floor up in the grand green-gilt lobby they fixed the Series over turtle soup and Pernod. Out front one of them hired heavies turned his gun on himself and sprayed the glass doors with Chicago paint.

The basement do like her little nightcaps.

Up and down between the parts of the world the brass-stamped dumbwaiters never stop. Bellhops like archangels bring eggs and honey from the heavenly farm to the sleepy kittens lying soft like the Flood never came. The kitchens turn out six tries at gluttony a day, silver domes and gold tureens. Up out of the underground kingdom flow diamond necklaces, ruby diadems, controlling stock in this and that, morphine like a quicksilver dream, laudanum like white honey, and the infinite, all-forgiving bubble-sea of wet-hot happy juice—don't mind the iodine, darling. You hardly even taste the kerosene. Up in heaven they call it drinking the soda pop moon. In that jazz-hearted Midgard called the Artemisia it's panther sweat. And down at the bottom of the world if you ask for coffin varnish you'll get what you're looking for.

One man rules it all, even when he's not there, even when he's back home counting money and bones. Oh, everyone knows who! If you saw him on the street you'd make a path for the shortest man in town, strutting along in his pixie-colored suits. The dapper never wears the same ones twice: tangerine, granny smith, grape popsicle, cotton candy. There's belladonna in his pockets, foxglove in his lapel, and a golden pistol in the lipstick linings of his jackets. The man powders his face like a dame at town, half an inch thick if it's none. Folks say a fella sliced up his face over a dance hall girl years back, scarred his cheeks something terrible. But it just ain't so. If he didn't pile it on, his boys would see he wasn't quite right—the color of his skin too blue, his ears too long, and I tell ya, if you look in his eyes too long you can see a ring of stars like toadstools at the bottom of their black.

Call him what you want: Scarface, Boss, Big Daddy, King of the Fairies and Lord of the Dead.

Most everyone around here just calls him Al.

1550

THERE'S A SAYING AMONG showgirls: this city only knows two kinds of stories. A girl comes to New York and a girl dies in New York. Well, I got a story to tell. Wanna make it interesting? What's the over/under on somebody leaving this book in a box? Leave your wager inside the dust-jacket, kittens.

YOU HAVE to work up a real lather to stand out among the sparklers at the Artemisia. When the kids look to be using up all the parties of the next hundred years in one summer, what's another passed-out sweetheart in silver fringe? What's one more gamine with her shoes danced to tatters? Nothing but a black bob on a pillow, a bathtub princess with her head in the sink.

Unless the girl was Zelda Fair.

A door popped up at the back of Zelda Fair's closet round about Thanksgiving-time. Room 1550. Nobody knew about the door, but everyone knew about Zelda. Well, they knew of her. The about came harder. Girl kept her lips tight on the subject of origins. Come from some nothing town in Pennsylvania or Missouri or Alabama to make it as a dancer or an actress or a writer, whichever came first. She drank like a Czar and sang like a broken squeezebox and danced like the Sugarplum Fairy cutting loose at last. Zelda was winter's best dame: pale and dark and thin with a shimmer of Christmas in her eye, a flash of New Year in her laugh. Every Tom, Dick, and Rockefeller threw themselves at her, showered her in emeralds like green candy, sent a regular parade of dresses in long grey boxes, the very opposite of Al's impish rags: Arctic midnight, storm-clouds, frost, pure 12-year aged starlight. If the It-girl didn't show up to your hop, you might as well just have a glass of warm milk go to bed early. And for a minute, not a little more and not a little less, Zelda was the It that never quit.

Zelda F couldn't afford that flat all on her lonesome, oh no. Three other sparrows had their first and last on the lease: Olive, Opal, and Oleander. Olive Bay made her scratch in the Follies, high-kicking her spike-heels against the North Star till her calves looked like them faces out on Easter Island. Opal Lunet sewed up shine for half the hotel to shimmy in. After a year in the Artemisia she'd handled so much glitter her fingertips would sparkle till she died—and then her grave-dirt dazzled, too. And Miss Oleander Coy had herself a blue mouth. Little stains at the edges of her raspberry lips where she put her pen when she was thinking, which was always. She told the town what to do and where to go—the acid girl, the bitterest critic ever to clench a column in each fist. And God help her if any of those nice rich theater folk find out the hard-to-please heart they're dying to win belongs to a black girl. A byline's as good as a mask.

They came to town: Olive and Opal high-tailing it from the boardwalks, Atlantic City and Virginia Beach. Guess they couldn't stand one more popcorn lunch between telling fortunes and dancing in a pretty glass box. Only Oleander was home-grown, Harlem first and Harlem last and Harlem the only room in her heart.

You might think, when four girls get up to living together, a nice fat kitty-cat just puffs into existence on their favorite chair, already fitted out with a crooked tail, a missing ear, a disinclination to catch anything not already put in a china bowl for them at suppertime, and a name like Tiger or Smoky or Mr. Puss-Boots. Not so for 1550. But it's true when Ollie turned the key with a suitcase and a soup-pot in her saddlebags, the apartment was already occupado. Some scoundrel'd left their pet behind— back then the odder flat was the one without some zoo escapee noshing off the oatmeal pot. The poor beast flapped and squawked and banged around the empty walls and fresh, clean windows, in and out of the bedrooms like a wicked boy, whack on the ceiling, smash on the stove-top. Funniest looking bird you ever saw! Big as a kindergartner, beak like a pink scimitar, feathers on top like the cream on milk and shiny as a black satin ball-gown on bottom. The ornithologist in 1523 gave them the scoop later on, and the scoop was called Pelecanus Conspicillatus. The Perceptive Pelican of the Southern Hemisphere.

But they did name him Puss-Boots.

Room 1550 was only ever quiet from 3:30 am to just around 5, when even those four had to show their necks to sleep. Then it was Olive first to the clock, singing scales around her toothbrush, up and stretching her long legs on a stick of hickory she'd bolted to the kitchen wall while sucking down black coffee with one hand and reading the latest book Ollie had told her redeemed the whole idea of writing a story from start to finish with the other. Puss-Boots stretched with her, his neck, his bill, his long legs, but never his wings, careful as a girl fresh out of finishing school, him being so big that opening up his great fat wings would knock over the milk jugs, the phonograph, the teacups, the side table near the sofa, and probably the sofa, too. Somebody'd trained that pelican to be downright dainty.

Opal hit the tile next, still mostly asleep while she fed a whirl of silk through her rat-a-tat machine, chasing a river of thread through the teal. Ollie punched in with the cymbal-whack of her typewriter by the alley-side window while a happy neon sign six stories down flashing Hobart and Sons' Fine Smokables got its purple light all tangled up in her eyelashes. And sooner or later all this racket would thump Zelda Fair out of her linen, wandering out naked as a painting and straight to the gin-jar: the Artemisia's favorite breakfast. By eight a.m. the bellhop, just as bright as a rooster in his cap and brass, would ding the bell with fresh eggs from the rooftop and a pot of honey on account of him being sweet on all four of them, but one in particular. See if you can guess.

Zelda boiled them up hard for her sisters and toasted bread, if they had any, over the gas range, yawning like she might get her mouth around the whole world. And before she laid out the 1550 blue-light special, she'd say now, there'll be no more Zelda Mummying you once I find my Goodies, my darling O's. You'll have to eat 'em raw.

That was how Miss Fair called whatever talent she would, soon, can't be long now, turn out to have all locked up at the bottom of her. Her gentlemen-friends laughed and patted her hair and told her not to fuss about it, she was perfect at being Zelda and they'd keep her in eggs and diamonds forever. But not our Z, not her. She wanted to be Good. Not just Good, but Good at

Something. She coaxed her Goodies like a fussy cat, whispering for them, kissing for them, leaving out milk in the hall. She tried something new every Tuesday so that she couldn't possibly miss her Goodies when they showed up.

This week was sonnets. She wore fourteen bracelets on her right arm and drizzled her poems in honey over her darlings' morning toast. Last week was lion-taming. A beardy fella down on the fifth floor who owned three entire separate theatres below 50th St kept a big old circus cat named Marlowe, who still trotted the boards for the odd Tempest or Midsummer or any show cheap enough to rely on a grandpa-lion snoozing upstage left for excitement. Zelda put her head in Marlowe's mouth and took it out again over and over. Marlowe sat patiently on his green velvet armchair like the cat was at the dentist. He was an awful good sport about it, but she couldn't call it a triumph. Zelda was viciously honest with herself. Can't say you're a lion tamer when the four-legged carpet's already tamed. He did bite her once, when he fell asleep with her still using his tongue for a pillow and his poor jaw just went slack. Didn't hurt a bit. She just pried herself loose, curled up between his paws, and helped herself to his nap.

Miss Fair put her head in all kinds of things last week, I tell you what.

THE DOOR in Room 1550 up and invited itself into Zelda Fair's boudoir like everyone else—plain as you please, no different than the door out into the hallway, just smaller. Knocker and knob gleaming fine. Maybe it smelled a little like fresh paint. Maybe the keyhole was a little dinged up like they get when their owner keeps on coming home so soused they gotta scrape that key over the brass like butter and toast before they can figure where the grease goes. Maybe it came up to a girl's waistline, but no higher than the hip-slinger length they hung back in '24. That door settled on in like anybody else. Locked itself up tight behind a curtain of icicle-dresses and stockings thin as coughing.

And ever since that door moved in, Zelda's checked out.

1801

UP IN 1801, THAT fellow who played Robin Hood at the flickies threw a New-New Year's bash to cause fits. January is so depressing after New Year, he moaned. Nothing but slush and onion soup and shredded streamers. Can't have it! Not at the Artemisia. Let's give January a good sock in the jaw and a double-slug of bourbon on her way out, shall we?

Robin Hood knew how make Sherwood jangle and all the merry men shimmy till their spats popped. I'm telling you, Portuguese trapeze-swinging triplets flew from chandelier to chandelier and four separate barons—one newspaper, one copper, one railroad, and one baritone sax—played poker on the floor with their socks off. Some bright-blood jazz-daddy pounded that monster grand piano with a tiger-skin draped over his shoulders, striped head on his head, teeth bouncing on his skull like his fingers on the keys, while a ballerina with a missing pinky finger plinked out the high notes for him with her perfect pointed toes. Maid Marian came with two flamingos named Cliquot and Strawberry, one on each arm like a pair of beaux. Even the curtains had dates—that lump in the velvet over there is none other than a lady blackmailer and a fella who's Papa started a whole religion. It's true if I'm a day old. Nobody came without their sequins roaring. Hell, without sparkle, you were as good as naked in the Artemisia. And oh yes, King Gin and Queen Whiskey and their little bouncing baby Champagne showed up first and left last. Screwing in the bathroom, dancing on the tabletops, giggling on the rug.

Now, you know those royals weren't supposed to show their face in company back then. Some fine little dandies out in Washington waggled their fat fingers and said: don't you go doing that nasty old thing mankind's loved better'n babies since before the Egyptians ever hearda eyeliner. And we crossed our fingers behind our backs and said yes, sir, Mr. Fancy Hats. You sure do know what's best for us. And as soon as those temperate backs were turned, out came every flask and jug and barrel and milk bottle, upturned down every gullet. Nobody drank like we drank, not since beer was new and scotch was still some ambitious peat bog's pipe dream. The second it wasn't allowed, liquor turned magic on us. Sweeter, stronger, bitterer, better. I suppose that might have been the wood alcohol, but it didn't matter. Screw opium, snuff can go hang—who can get me a beer? A little rum, mister? How 'bout a swallow of red wine? For my nerves, you understand. We chased it like leprechaun gold, chased it down alleys and up six, ten, thirteen stories, chased it out of the city and underground. Every Granny who didn't think twice about her evening sherry in 1919, in 1920 knew somebody who knew somebody and might shank somebody with her sewing scissors if she didn't get her bottle on the sharp. If it could rot, we made it booze. Peaches and limes and cherries and apples and gasoline and iodine and Lysol and the wood off the church pews. Slurp it up, call it friend, hold it tight, keep it safe.

But in the Artemisia, you could always get a nip of the good stuff. Something real: absinthe, Pernod, Lillet, Cabernet, Rhum Louisiane, however many malts would please you, gin that had once actually met a juniper tree. Al kept it coming and nobody asked how and his only rule was: share. Be warm, be innocent, open your everything, speak easy. Share.

Robin Hood already knew that song. Share it round, Prince John's bag, King Richard's ransom, a mason jar of slivovitz like the plums of heaven. And round it went, round a room of shimmy and shine and cigarette girls singing soulful past two a.m. and flamingo shit on the Moroccan rug. Boy, I'da thought they'd crap pink, wouldn't you, Dougie? Guess not, Viv, guess not. Just the kind of scene Zelda lived to die for, just the kind of room she could smell winding up before the first cocktail cocked.

And she was there—old Robin Hood would've turned in his tights if Miss Z had put on cold cream and curled up with *Amazing Stories* and a cup of warm milk. She sauntered on in just as the jugglers got going, her bob so perfect it could've cut her cheekbones, wearing one of Olive's dresses, a spangled blue cupcake that showed her thighs all the way up to her soul. She kissed Robin Hood. She kissed Maid Marian. She kissed the lady blackmailer and the prophet's son and the piano player and the ballerina and one of the flamingos and three different poor boys who'd never see their plays on stage.

And by ten o'clock she was lying on the sideboard, sparkling knees drawn up to her chin, salmon tarts near her head and pineapple upside-down cake near her feet, sleeping hard as that sad sack who pricked a spindle when the world was young.

2064

SO WHO RUNS IT all? Who built this cuckoo clock world ticking away the nights on 72nd St?

Oh, darling, this is the Copper King's Palace, his favorite daughter—and the only one who still loves him even the littlest bit.

Caspar Anson Slake, whose Daddy never met a mountain he couldn't suck the copper off of or a soul he couldn't find a way to hating. Couldn't stand children, Papa Slake, his own least and last. I heard he left his cash to Caspar because everyone pissed him off so hard and so regular he only made a will once he figured the best way to sucker punch somebody or nine on the way out. Papa S twigged to his middle son's ambitions of running off to Switzerland to make clocks in a cave on the Matterhorn or some hogwash, while the eldest and youngest wanted to be CEOs the way folks used to want to be emperors. Fine and dandy—Caspar got the whole sandwich, along with a postscript saying if he chucked it to his brothers the Church would clean up and they'd all be left asking after soup downtown.

The outside of the Artemisia preens with copper. Polished like a penny in a loafer. Caspar sits in his penthouse like a roosting hen, clucking over the only clock he ever set to ticking. Named it for his baby sister who went red in the face and died at seven months old rather than say one word to that family.

His wife sits up there, too, Pearl de Agosti y Candela, this tiny 22-year old spit of a Cuban-Catalan child, the most sculpted face in New York for about a year, give or take. She's Justice at City Hall, St. Barbara at St. John's, Spring in a seashell in Central Park. Rumor goes her uncle's a duke in Spain—or was it a baron in Italy? Caspar had 45 years on his ticket and a hanker for the face he saw on the statue of Temperance outside his favorite scotch-and-cockery club. The only thing he really liked about his Daddy's money was how nobody ever said no to him anymore. You know how this song goes. Man says marry and just like the worst magic trick in the world—bang! smash!—a girl's wearing white even though it's never been her color.

Girl Pearl had about a thousand sisters, all living it up better than she knew how, fucking silent film actresses and boxing and piloting airplanes just to show girls could do it, too. Sucking the world out of an egg cup while Pearl stewed in her birdcage, missing her sculptors, hating her kid, whining, puking Little Cass, who never asked to have parents who only read about love in books. Pearl was only nice to Cass on Tuesdays, for an hour, between four and five when she gave him chocolate and read to him from a big old fairy book full of stories about bad mothers.

Don't you hate her already? I sure do.

All her husband's animals made her sneeze—Mr. Slake up there started the policy on pets in Artemisia apartments. First it was a Mongolian hunting eagle by the name of Ogedei, who naturally had to have his own bedroom. Honestly, woman, do you expect a bird like that to sleep in a coop on the roof like an idiot pigeon? Then she had to suffer a couple of red foxes relaxifying on the fainting couch, and later in Little Cass's bed. Then came the peacock and the bobcat and the baby black bear—but once Gogol the jaguar moved in, Pearl threw a fit you could hear in Harlem. The great diaspora. You know what happened to that sweet little bear. He kept growling I love you I love you back at Pearl the whole way up to the roof and she wanted to give in but she just couldn't do it. A trombonist took in the flamingos. A raggedy lion, already paid for but not yet landed, was quietly re-routed to Caspar's buddy Wiley Hachett down on five, where he let girls practice taming him if they asked nicely. Caspar's three seals ended up in the lobby fountain, splashing around and barking at the buttresses. But Pearl was stuck with Ogedei, and Gogol, and the foxes, who loved Little Cass like a chicken bone. The kidlet named them Boo and Roo. Caspar plumped for Hannibal and Hasdrubal, but his boy didn't care and couldn't say those damn words anyhow.

Pearl's writing a book. Slowly, carefully, in the corners when nobody can see her, in the wee hours when nobody's bawling for her. It's not a good book, but it sure is fun to read. Pearl doesn't have the knack of changing what happens to her into something brighter, wilder, thicker. She doesn't know the trick of cutting up what really happens and stitching it together with what didn't or couldn't or shouldn't happen and rat-a-tatting a selvedge edge on time so that this thing that went down when she was in pigtails sits right up flush next to the hurt she found when she was twenty. She can only call things straight and flat, as they are, in the order they ordered, no piddling around. Her protagonist is Mrs. Paige Stokes who has a husband called Carlyle and a kid named Little Ly. Her book is a house with glass walls and her the only cat inside.

Now, that sort of style is all right in moderation, but the trouble is, Pearl was a society lady now. The Copper Queen. And the Copper Queen can't swear, no sir. She can't spit or get drunk or wander around her own damn flat naked or laugh too loud. Her sculptors let her do all that and loved her better when she did. Good Lord, but who doesn't love a Minerva half-cracked on bourbon, telling dirty jokes and laughing at her own farts? Christ, she missed farting! The man who made her Temperance used to let go like a stevedore, and she'd blast right along with him. Now she has to hold it in until she's alone and can let her tinny little society stinkers out in a locked powder room, giggling like her rear could tell jokes. So she held it in all day, the swearing, the spitting, the drinking, the farting, until she could be alone with her book and it all came whistling, bubbling, splattering out.

Mrs. Rockaway joined Pearl de Agosti y Candela y Slake for tea every second Wednesday. On this hot-trotting subject, Mrs. S writes: Mrs. Rockaway came round for tea at 3:15 in the afternoon. She asked to see Little Cass but he thinks she smells like dead squirrels and eagle's ass, so he wouldn't come out of his room. Finally, my boy shows some sense. Mrs. Rockaway said her son is starting Yale in the fall. Mrs. Rockaway says Steel is King and they get richer every time they take a shit. Mrs. Rockaway is fucking her son's long-cocked friend from the rowing squad, but she thinks I don't know. Mrs. Rockaway is a hell-bitch with a brain like old steak and her teeth are yellow. Truthfully, she's only here to get her biweekly booze, but Mrs. Rockaway feels obligated to me socially because Caspar crossed piss-streams with her husband sometime before the dawn of man. Additionally, she is a fat bear-cunt of a whore who knows I have smashing cakes in the icebox and wants to annex them. Nothing goes with a hippo's serving of Canadian gin like chocolate cake. And the Yale rowing squad. Lux et veritas, wouldn't you say, Mrs. R?

Mrs. Slake looks up from her typewriter (a spectacular custom-job blood-red Underwood with mother-of-pearl keys and a carriage release that used to be part of some swish pirate flintlock Caspar had lying around like it was no big thing. Pearl treats her Underwood like a car. After all, it's the only thing that gets her anywhere).

The jaguar watches her from the top of an armoire that holds Caspar's collection of Bronze Age knives. His eyes shine in the evening like tumblers of rum.

1415

ZELDA FAIR JUGGLES FOUR or five marriage proposals at once in a good month. See her throw them in the air, clubs, torches, plates spinning up on sword-tips, soft-shoeing it through the only dance a girl gets. She don't say no, she don't say yes, she just keeps on spinning 'cause if she stops…well, the plates'll be fine and the swords, too, they'll just keep going round and round while she falls and breaks into a million bitty pieces.

Sorry, chiclet. I did that dance, too, and it's a pile of shit on the bill, a pile of shit when the curtain goes up, and a pile of shit when it goes down. Shit is the one thing in this world that'll never leave your side.

Lucky Zelda's Daddy was a judge. A regular Rhadamanthus of the great American Delta. And her mother was Minerva Fair, who wanted to be an actress but the world said nope, be a lady instead, and she said no thank you please, and there ain't nothing like a goddess disappointed to teach a girl how to wait and how to choose.

Let's look at the boys wrapped up under Miss Z's Christmas tree this year! Bows and bangles and spangles and ribbons—Santa himself got blinded by the gleam! In 1415, there's Thomas Germain, who never met an oil rig that didn't wanna curl up at his feet like an Airedale. Tommy Dear makes promises like little boys make mudpies. The stage, the screen, the page, the cradle. All she has to do is cough and an ermine cape appears. If she catches a cold, she catches sapphires. Rich men are magicians, and that's the very end. They think everyone else is a magician, too, which is why Thomas turns Zelda's laugh into a pre-nup and her any-old-Tuesday Charleston into a baby already born and snoozing.

In Room 1940, Josiah Shadduck pines like a Canadian forest. His grandaddy knew the Yukon in a Biblical way and every kitten in the Shadduck basket gets a little gold nugget put under their tongue at their Christening so they won't forget the taste of money. Josie looks like a gold mine: big and rosy and stubborn and just as much filth as the good stuff. He thinks Zelda is the water who'll run through him and leave him clean. She never wears his gold necklaces, not even the tiara with a pink diamond shaped like a wildflower stuck in it. She keeps his loot in a box under her bed. A girl who knows every other day's a rainy one stocks up on slickers.

In 988, William Hessen-Hyde bides his time. He's almost a Duke and when his uncle kicks it he'll be all of one. Girls like Dukes,.he's been assured by the whole wide world. All he has to do is sit still and be a Duke and Zelda will weigh Duchessing heavier than any little glass another beau can toss her way. Billy hedges his bets, though. He's gonna have to high-tail it back to Germany to get in on that Duke game, and he knows he's gotta sweeten the pot for a New York girl. Gave our Zelda a ruby brooch: a rooster snacking on the crest of his house. And he's promised her a forest all her own, with a damn good lake inside. She can't wear it socially, but it can wear her. Just as soon as death makes an honest man of him. He's made himself a little vow—not a drop of booze until he can put her name on those trees.

"I wish I had half your boys," Olive Bay says while she stretches her hamstrings on the sideboard in Room 1550.

Zelda and Oleander and Opal play poker. They deal in their pelican Mr. Puss-Boots, who interferes with the cards but can't get the hang of betting. Zelda lays down a Jack for the house.

"You don't," she says.

"I could stand being a Duchess," Opal opines. "All the silk I could stitch. And cakes for tea every damn day of the week."

Zelda lays down a three of hearts. "Tommy said he'd make me a star."

"Isn't that what you want?" asks Olive Bay, bluffing for everything.

"I said: what if I'm not any good? And he said: who cares?"

"That bastard," Ollie says, and she's not making fun. They all know. Who cares is them, all of them. They care so much.

"I'm gonna be good at something besides marrying, darlings. Besides, I don't want them. I don't even wanna screw them, how am I gonna marry them?"

Mr. Puss-Boots puts his feathered head on her knee. He hasn't got anything to offer. But he'd bring her fish and guard her eggs if she gave him half a chance.

THEN THERE'S Frankie Key, of course. Down on two. But Zelda doesn't know about him yet.

212

SECOND FLOOR: STAFF DIGS. Six to a suite unless you're management, but a suite's a suite. Nobody does much but sleep down on two anyhow. You don't get to kick up your feet with a pipe and a British novel round these parts. Bellhops hit duty like a punching bag at 3 a.m. Concierges swap out like the royal guard at noon and midnight, front desk girls in lipstick and victory rolls run nine-hour shifts of flash-teeth-when-you-smiles and and-your-key-sirs. Kitchens never do close, and cleaning never does stop. Uniforms so green you'd swear they were grown in a Swiss meadow hang like six smart ghosts in each parlor, brass buttons polished, caps jaunty even without a head to hold them up or a hand to tip them.

Frankie Key is an egg-hop by day and a pneumatic boy by night. He shares 212 with a pair of twins out of Texas everyone calls Nickel and Dime, a Vermont college boy name of Murray Keen, a preacher's son born under the sorry name of Hallelujah Barnes, though he's shortened that up to Hal now, and Enzo Bacchi, a painter from some nothing town in the Swiss Alps who covers every hidden surface of the room with miniature cosmic ragtime parades, goblins and gargoyles and gamines and gallants dancing under the lip of every windowsill, the ledge of every counter-top, the under-slats of all six beds, the back of the medicine cabinet, even the inside of the broken faucet in the kitchen, wherever the boss-men won't see it when they come on inspection. Room 212 has a secret Hieronymus shindig shaking down all over itself, and sometimes her boys lie flat on the parlor floor, six heads spread in a star, looking up at the underside of Enzo's heart.

All those sweet boys used to work as caddies on some rich man's great huge lawn, so that's what most everyone called them. Those Caddies, ain't they swell?

Now, Frankie, he was born in Minnesota but mostly got to walking and talking in Buffalo, that upstate snow-show with barely a canal and a train-line to rub together. Some eighth of a cousin of his wrote a song you probably know. Daddy was a pharmaceutical man, selling Well-Being door to door. Mama was a greengrocer's daughter with moles on her middle knuckles, all ten of them, like little pinpricks for marionette strings. Sent their boy to Catholic school to learn what boys learn there, which is mostly how not to be a Catholic ever again. Missed the war by a hair—Armistice did her cannonball splash while Frankie was learning how to march and salute and un-rifle, then re-rifle, then un-rifle a rifle in some swamp in Alabama. The war he didn't fight sticks on him like shit on a shoe. He can still smell it, even though nobody else can, even though his sole is clean.

Frankie, he loved his green-hand Mama like the rest of us loved Kentucky rye, and that's the truth. Every Friday he put a little lavender envelope into the gloved hand of Mr. Raspail F. Bayeux, head Concierge, stamped for Buffalo with love. She did love purple, Mrs. Key. These days you and I and anybody would pay all our little pennies for one of those envelopes, for his sharp, bright, sly paragraphs of mother-love and city-woes. But Buffalo takes no prisoners.

So let's all be Frankie for a spell. Up we go at the crack of better-dead-than-out-of-bed, two hours sleep if it was a minute, one leg into our billiard-green trousers, then the other. Shirt, coat, hat-strap tight under our chin, gloves, shoes slicker than glass. Into the lift, screen shut tight, and up, up, up through all the sleeping continents of the world inside the Artemisia, the only world that counts. Up, darling, always up. The soul of Frankie Key points up and its the only direction that seems friendly. Down'll getcha if you get sleepy and happy with what you got. So up we go. Up past the Green Tabernacle restaurant on four where the day's first bread is busy rising and the coffee-troughs are already brimming. Up past that mess on seven with the dueling pharmacists who have to give serious think-space every day to whether or not to shoot each other in the hall. Up past the torch-singer on ten crying through her scales. Up past the sixteenth floor, where the weird wizardry of room assignments had either fallen asleep on the job or shown up early for work, depending on your attitude. This is where the front desk dumped all the bookbinders, librarians, novelists (but not short story writers, columnists, or playwrights), editors, illustrators, and two genuine muses on tap for the convenience of all, Lily Greer, the great Vaudeville boy-dresser and scissor-swallower, and Dandelion Bruno, pretty Dandy Brute who killed a fella in St. Louis 'cause he stole a rose out of the boy's lapel. On sixteen all the doors stand open and every parlor is choking on books. You can walk right in and borrow anything you like, sit in a nice chair and peruse yourself a fine leather volume. If you have the time. Which we do not. Up past the penthouses on twenty and onto the roof, the green dewy roof all full of chickens and goats and morning.

Frankie likes it up here. You can see the whole city, lights still out, quiet as a church. He named the chickens after ancient queens—it's the sort of thing Frankie likes to imagine telling folk he did when he was young, so he does it. Boudicea, Theodora, Elizabeth, Mathilda, Antoinette—but they're all white Delawares so he can't tell them apart anyway. Come on, Messalina, he calls the hundreds of them all together, time to send your heirs to the slaughter. And he fills up his baskets with warm brown eggs while they purr and mew and chuckle, more like kittens than the great old dinosaur-cousins they are. Enzo'll be up to milk the goats later, and Nickel and Dime to hack of hunks of honeycomb from the hives while they sing old cowboy songs to Rutherford, who thinks, privately, that those boys can't sing for shit. And egg-boys, more egg-boys, a dozen and more, to bring down breakfast to the little nations of the Artemisia, free of charge, golden and rich as the sun on a day nobody's fucked up yet.

Let's all feel our hearts crammed in Frankie's chest, feel us churning up, wheeling, bonging, squishing blood down to our undersides as the lift drops down and the fifteenth floor gets nearer, and with the fifteenth floor Room 1550, and with Room 1550 all those beautiful girls like princesses dancing through their shoes, but especially Zelda Fair, opening the door with that sleepy, heavy, sharp, hot look her eyes have, saying the same thing every day like it's the first day and she's never seen an egg before.

"Oh! You shouldn't have."

And what's Frankie's night shift? Never you mind. Mr. Slake signs his bellboy checks every month, but Frankie's other job doesn't tally in that dandified ledger with such nice, gold-tipped pages. He punches in at 9 pm on the tenth floor, half way to heaven and halfway to the pit. What he does there pays a whole sight better than chicken farming. And it's Al who signs those notes, with a signature like a scream in the dark.

872

GOT ALL THAT? HAVE I dramatised our personae to the hilt? I know it's tough to keep all the cards in order, my chickies, but I'm doing my best. It's ok. I wouldn't leave you in the lurch without a flashlight. Just shine it on over here. Zelda and Ollie and Opal and Olive and the pelican Mr. Puss-Boots, Frankie and Enzo and Murray Keen and Nickel and Dime with their matching dimples, Caspar and poor pissed off Pearl and their Little Cass who thinks blue blood smells like fox farts, Gogol the jaguar, Ogedei the eagle, Marlowe the swell lion, Lily Greer with her vaudeville drag show, and Al, dandy Al in his cherry-cream suit with rosemary in his lapel, Al, who don't care for the light, waiting down there in the basement for us to come to him. Don't worry. He'll keep.

Harold Kloburcher shacks up in Room 872 with a lady who isn't his wife, but she isn't not his wife, either. Miss Georgiette's actually married to some ether-man down in Baltimore, but she can't stand the sight of him and he can't stand the sight of her and there's only so much marriage you can huff through a wet rag before somebody hits the road. But Georgiette and Harold have their sympatico locked up tight in a jar and they've been playing house for coming on ten years now.

They're in the same line of work, see. Harry's a locksmith and Georgie's a madam. They both let you in when you're shut out. Oh, Georgie wouldn't call it that. But everybody knows where to go when you want somebody lying under you who knows how to look like they want to be there. And if you're a little short on rent and shorter still on the lessons your mama gave you before you lit out for the big city, just head on down to 872 and tell Miss G you've got a powerful thirst for some of her darjeeling, sugar, no lemon. She's got a painting of dogs hunting a unicorn on the wall over the fireplace. Opens on a hinge like the door to paradise. On the backside she's hung up a broadsheet with all the names and prices and dates available, split into a Girls column and a Boys column, and whaddya know but they're about the same length. Georgie wouldn't use your real name—she's a class act all the way according to her own self, and she learned from her locksmith hunk the sacred trust that goes along with knowing how to get a key in anywhere you like. Discretion, pets. The State Department has fewer code names than Georgiette Boursaw's unicorn painting. All out of fairy tales, on account of her sweet, soft childhood in Albany, when she loved to read about maidens and towers and horses and dragons, before the man with the fabulous gas and the big slurry fists came to show her how to dance the Sleeping Beauty rag.

So this week, which is Christmas week 1924, if you're into that sort of thing, you can have Cinderella for six dollars fifty but keep it out of her mouth, thanks. Or Snow White for a fiver, though you can't kiss her. Rapunzel's going for ten bucks even, but it's a bargain for a contortionist who likes to be choked. Prince Charming will cost you seven, Joringel four, poor wee lamb chop can't outlast a lit match but oh, those blue eyes will kill you dead. And Clever Jack wants a prince's ransom, twelve smackers, but you can do anything you like and he's hung like a Stone Age statue. Oh, you could get it all for less out on the town, but why bother when the Artemisia will send up room service nice and neat?

Everyone gets a new name in the Artemisia. The front desk is Ellis Island backwards—come Elizabeth Smith and find yourself Licorice Lizzy of the Cigarette Soul before you hit the elevator.

So imagine Miss Georgie's eyes when Zelda Fair comes knocking shy, big eyes all haunted-hollow, wearing her respectable clothes, a grey dress with buttons instead of rosettes and rhinestones. Georgie knows that hollow look. That look that says golly gee ma'am I never done this before but I love this damn heap of bricks and I'm just a little short this month... And the money she could get for Zelda, without even haggling! She's already poured tea and plated out iced cookies and named the girl Gretel in her head before Zelda clears her throat and twists her hands and asks to see Mr. Kloburcher instead. Too bad, Georgie. So sad.

Harold feels mighty pleased to be called on. He works locks for the hotel and he works on the quiet, too, on the side—sometimes a body doesn't want the front desk knowing their business. He likes his hush-hush jobs best. He feels like a spy, on one knee, fiddling the tumblers till secrets pop free. He looks Miss Z up and down and figures he'll make a roast chicken tonight, to feed Georgie's disappointment. But now Zelda Fair's looking at him with that face, that tea-cake chin, that gin-sloe smile, and her throat's all red above her collarbone, which is, Harold guesses, how somebody like her blushes when they blush at all.

"Tell us all your troubles, sweetheart," he says in his best plummy grandfather voice that practically lights a pipe with its vowels. "You wanna try locksmithing this week? Little fingers like yours, could be your Goodies in spades."

Zelda laughs, but it's a little, short laugh, the kind that isn't really a laugh at all. Just punctuation. "Sometimes funny things happen in this world, don't they, Mr. K? I mean, the world's so damn big everything's bound to happen that can happen, and probably some things that can't."

"I suppose so."

"And when funny things happen, you just have to go along, don't you? Because they might never happen again and you'll have missed the joke of it, missed the fun, and then when you're old and your kittens ask you what you did when the world had its glad rags on, you won't have nothing to say, will you?"

"Honey, I don't follow you."

"You need a drink, baby girl?" Georgiette asks, just as sweet as a pie filled with aunties. "I think we got some anise in the cupboard."

Zelda takes it in a little green crystal glass and for a second she's so dazzled by the winter light streaming through the window streaming through the glass and streaming onto her knuckles like emerald licorice rings that she forgets to talk and her mind whangs off thinking about how anise ought to be black, or at lease purple, the way licorice is, but it's as white as a window pane…

Georgie's talk bubbles all over, bicarbonate of gossip. "I got it straight from the source, no need to worry, lovie. Nothing foul in there. Harry, did you hear three people died of that ginger poison at Bill Radner's jake joint last week? I don't even look at the stuff unless I saw the man downstairs tap it with his own hand. You drink up, Zelda. Your color's out."

"I'm sorry!" Zelda snaps back into Room 872 and shoots back her licorice like water. "I'm sorry. I feel like I'm made of paper these days. Gotta pile rocks on me to keep me from flying away."

"Red meat," Georgie prescribes. She knows from paper girls. Does she ever. "Red meat and brown liquor. Roots you to the earth. Keeps you hot. I've got some steaks in the icebox, dear. I'll wrap them up for you. Just fry them with a little butter, two minutes a side. Eat up all the fat, too, suck the bones. I'll know if you don't."

Zelda tries to refuse but Georgiette would mother a hole in the wall. That's what comes of Albany and Buffalo and slurping down a thousand stories where nobody's got a mother worth spitting on. She comes back with a brown paper parcel and a little round silver flask. Zelda's in the middle of saying:

"...up in my room. Just come look. I can pay. I can! I fixed Mrs. Acosta's stove last week. I'm flush. Well, golly! My Daddy taught me how to make things work when they quit on you. He wouldn't have anyone saying he raised a Helpless Hattie. That's what he called girls who only knew how to be pretty. Now, being pretty's plenty hard, but nobody's Daddy since the dawn of time ever cottoned on to that—there I go again, blowing away! Just come, Mr. K. Come look and if you can't do it no harm's done."

Harold the spy lives for a hard lock. Georgie hands over her love wrapped in brown paper. Blood seeps through the bottom. They don't see it drip, but they feel it.

1090

FRANKIE KEY SPIFFS HIMSELF up real good for the evening. He takes a change of clothes up to the tenth floor. He gets off early tonight. Free and clear by midnight and he feels just as fine as candy about it. Al gave him a new suit, and boy, a suit from Al is prettier than a girl's ballgown. No boy of mine should have to slum a party in a paper bag like yours, he said. Where'd you get it, you uncle's funeral when you were fourteen? Come 'ere, kid. You look like a fifty-pound nun in a ten-pound habit.

Frankie touches it while he sets out the tools of this particular job. She'll be impressed. Anybody would be. The suit's this kind of grey that's barely grey at all, but lavender and blue and a little green, too. It shines a little when you move in it, and he does plan to move. It's got a tie the hot, heady color of the bougainvillea in his mother's garden way back. Ruby chip cufflinks and fennel flowers in the buttonhole. And if those shoes aren't actual goatskin, Frankie here will eat his book.

Oh yeah, Frankie's writing a book. Everybody's writing a book in this joint. It's the thing to do. Furrow your brow over pages and pull your best Keats-face, your best long-tooth Joyce-mug and the girlies just fall all over you. The lads, too. It's a 100% kind of magic, works on everyone. Make me a character, won't you? I was just born for the page. Make me art. Make me alive. Make me real 'cause you're only real if somebody's talking about you, and fiction's the best kind of gossip there is. Every time some sad sack in the Artemisia thinks say, I oughta write a book, an angel falls flat on its face on 42nd Street and gets a ticket for jaywalking.

But Frankie's not bad. Mostly he's been writing detective stories up till now. It does nice things to his mind, like working a puzzle backwards, pulling out pieces one at a time until he's the only one who knows the picture. Besides, stories that start with a dead girl sell. He doesn't like that. His mother wouldn't like it. But it's true. He'll try something else, someday. Something smart and cold and hard in all the right places. He just hasn't found his big thing yet. He will. He knows it. Boys always know their big damn deal is right around the corner, sucking cigarettes and panting their name. But right now the murder racket snags him bylines and smart's not doing the trick. So up with blood and down with melancholy! Yes sir, hack those throats, fire those guns, furrow those Holmesy brows! It's easy to be lazy when lazy keeps you in gin. Frankie's not monogamous when it comes to detectives. No Poirot or Spade for him. He likes to be a new man every time he punches a typewriter. And honestly, his night-gig will keep him in stories till he's out of teeth and time.

And what's his gig? Frankie's a tube-man.

When Mr. Slake rustled himself up a hotel, he kitted her out with the best and newest of everything. Why not? The best is better, isn't it? New beats old in everything but wine and compound interest. Frankie'd never seen anything like the tubes when he slid into home in that fine front lobby. Pneumatic tubes, all through the place like veins through an elephant, opening up into every room with little brass cubby-doors and long glass pipes. If you could see through walls, you'd see this fantastic glass spider hugging onto the whole damn castle. And in the pipes? Air rushing, rushing all the time, air so beefy it'll carry a capsule from one floor to another, a capsule like a crystal ball, stuffed with whatever you want. Messages, trinkets, lipstick handkerchiefs, tickets, keys, candies, paints, pens—but mostly messages. He has no idea how it works. It could be a great big green-assed genie puffing into a hookah in the basement for all he knows. Frankie doesn't use it himself—but he knows the score.

See, Al showed up on the roof one morning. Just leaning against the chicken coop in his cotton candy suit like it was the finest throne in England. He tossed an egg up in the air and caught it and said: heya, Frances, how'd you like to make some real scratch? And any Buffalo boy knows when the big man says he wants a favor you just better hop.

So, this is what Frankie does for Al: he sits in Room 1090, not even a suite, just a single halfway between the roof and the basement. And whenever a crystal ball comes flying up the chute, he grabs it, jots down what's inside in a big green book, then sends it back on its way. If it's a letter, he copies it out. If it's a trinket, he describes it down to the gold chain and the porcelain handle and records the to and the from. Everything passes through Room 1090. Everything goes in the book. Frankie has nice handwriting. Frankie has a tidy little heart. Frankie assumes he's not the only one. Some cat like him on every floor, most likely.

These are some of the things that pass through Frankie like a like that lady on the fortune telling card, passing water from one jug to another.

Send up the Matchstick Girl and Iron Hans tonight, won't you, Mme. Georgiette? After supper, if you please. —E. F. Rm 1216

You owe me twenty bucks on account I chewed off Bobby Smile's ear for you last week and if you don't pay up I could do yours for free. —J.W. Rm 401

Mr. Bessler, a fella got me in some awful trouble and he ain't never gonna marry me 'cause his name goes up in lights every night and mine goes down in the dirt. I got six dollars saved and I know you can do it quick. —S.A. Rm 244

I'll need a case of rum tonight, Raspy, four bottles champ. & two vermouth. Just a quiet night in with friends. —Q. T. L. Rm 1967

Don't you love me anymore? —O. C. Rm 1550

If you send me another letter I shall have you evicted. This one I shall burn. I advise you to do the same. —B. R. Rm 1388

Of course, baby. Of course I love you. Come down tonight. I'm sorry. —E.B. Rm 212

Miss Lily, I cannot abide another night without you. My wife is away. Come up. Wear your boy's clothes. I shall kiss your feet. I shall kiss your everything. —C.A.S. Rm 2064

1709

THE BIG PARTY'S ON seventeen tonight—a double birthday for King Lear and the Mad Mauler, a silver screen slickie and the heavyweight champion of the world. Though how the Big M crunched that poor bastard's face in Toledo nobody can figure. Unless somebody loaded down his gloves something special. Unless 1919 was a mighty fine year for crossing palms in the Artemisia lobby while the seals barked like three stupid fates with one beach ball between 'em. Never you mind, I guess.

By the time Frankie shows, it's gimlets and Gomorrah up there. The Slovenian tenor who made such a thumping glory of Carmen last month plays Apollo, zinging arrows from a serious mister of a bow, whacking his shots into the moose-head hanging over the elevator, popping the lights in the hall, telling filthy jokes about bear-fucking to girls on roller skates. His laugh blows through three octaves. Doors are flung open, people pouring in and out, the whole floor shaking, hopping, dancing, hollering. Through one door Frankie K can see a naked girl standing in a washtub pouring champagne over her head and reciting *The Rime of the Ancient Mariner* while everybody throws dimes over their shoulders like she's the goddamned Trevi Fountain. King Lear, wearing his prop crown, has Cordelia bent over a chest of drawers in the back bedroom, huffing Now, gods, stand up for bastards! while he does his big scene on her back.

On the floor in 1790, the Mad Mauler's own pad, there's six or seven cats playing dice on the rug. Frankie looks closer. It's no game he knows. Bone dice. Burned-in pips. One girl looks up at some player who's got fifty years over her and hisses: double five and the antelope burns, old man. Her face looks like she swallowed a limelight when she says it. Frankie shivers.

He taps antelope-girl's shoulder. She looks up at him, all milk of innocence.

"Have you seen Zelda?" he asks.

"Who?"

"Zelda. Zelda Fair. About this high, short black hair, smile like a punch in the gut?"

"Oh. No, Mister, I haven't seen her all night. I'm sure she's here, though. Who'd miss this out? At one o'clock the Mauler's gonna go a round with that fat man from the pictures. Don't you run off! You'll find her."

"I think I saw her in the washroom," grunts one of the other dice-jockeys, who just this morning bought the fastest race-horse in Australia and put him on a boat to California. "If you're missing a girl, always look in the washroom, I always say. The dame's choice locale for passing out, hopping up, getting hers, bawling like a dog or gossiping like a goddamn parakeet."

Frankie trips over a bottle of Pernod, a tophat, a wolfhound, a stone-drunk textile heir, and a child star with blond curls like cinnamon buns on his way to the bedroom-sized washroom of Room 1709. He expects the door to be locked but it swings open, not even latched. It's empty in there: pink tile with green chevrons, three oval mirrors with electric lights and gold frames to make your face a painting, hart's-tongue ferns in bronze vases. Panther-skin to dry your footsies. And a grand tub, lizard-clawfoot, hacked out of a hunk of malachite hauled all the way back from the Congo by a fella who said he was coming to cure malaria. Amethyst taps shaped like rhino-heads, one grimacing for cold, the other panting for hot. That's where he finds her, Zelda Fair, hiding out, lying in the bath in her oyster-shimmer dress, strings of black pearls floating in the water all around her, stockings shriveled round her toes, a flapper mermaid caught with her fins out.

"You're the boy with the eggs," she says all dreamy and cool. It's a voice she learned when she was young and learned good. A voice that doesn't give up a damn thing. A voice that sounds bare and silly and sleepy though it's the best armor she's got. Zelda doesn't let her real voice out to play anymore. It might tear her throat out. "You got any on ya?"

"What are you doing in the bath?" He blurts, when he meant to say I came to find you because you are perfect. Frankie hasn't got the smooth god gave a porcupine, but he meant to do better than that.

"I'm writing a novel," Zelda purrs. She adds in a giggle, a little dash of aren't I just the maddest thing you ever met? You wouldn't go thinking I'm serious, would you, darling? You wouldn't do that to me.

"That's not how you write a novel."

"Show's what you know, silly."

"Well, I do know, actually. I go for a typewriter, myself."

"Oh?" Zelda does this move in the tub, spinning around and turning over at the same time to come up over the lip of the thing and flash her eyes at Frankie, who has no defense against this sort of thing. Who does? The tub sparkles with green light. She sparkles, too. Zelda sparkles so good men think it's love. "Do tell."

"Mostly detective stories just at the moment." He rubs the back of his neck like some hick farmer confused over seed and before he can shut up he's spilling it all. "Before I joined up, I pounded out a whole book. If the war was gonna get me, I figured I'd leave something behind. Something real. Something good. Trouble was, it wasn't real or good. I'm still working on that part. The real and the good. But what I want, what I want, is to do something big. I'm gonna. I will. I'm gonna be famous. I can feel the books I might write just sitting under my ribs. Like another heart."

"Don't we all, honey? That's what I do professionally. Wait around for something big."

Frankie's heart does a foxtrot on his liver. "I think you're something big."

Zelda laughs her little-old-me laugh. "That's mighty sweet of you to say. But I'm not yet. Don't you just love Not-Yet? It's like waiting to be born. I could be anybody yet. I could be a ballerina or a swimming champion. Or a pocketwatch. Or a Christmas pudding. Or a jackal."

"Are you drunk?"

"Completely, darling." Zelda rests her chin on one dripping hand. "Jackals are really the cutest little things, did you know? It's only that they scream so. They scream like death coming for you right quick. That's why they're in the Bible, acting the fool. I think I'd be a fine jackal, if I put my mind to it."

It was not going Frankie's way. Talking to Zelda felt like talking to a radio. It talked back, but you couldn't call it a conversation.

"Don't be cross," she whispered, sliding into the water so only her eyes showed above the green stone tub. "I like to talk, is all. My Daddy always said a lady's gotta sit still and hush her mouth except for please and thank you and you don't say. But it's not fair to do that to a girl. Talking is the most fun you can have. Clothes on, clothes off, it's everything in the world. Don't you think you oughta do the only thing you can manage that animals can't just as often as possible? I suppose parrots can talk, too. But no one pays attention to a thing they say. And mostly, mostly, when I talk it's like being a parrot. Men say oh, aren't you clever and scratch me under my beak and give me treats. So I talk nonsense quite a little bit. Because it's fun. And they don't pay any attention anyhow. Only it's not really nonsense. It wouldn't be nonsense, if you knew me extra well."

I am here to tell you Frankie Key is a lost cause from here on out. If he ever had a hope of getting out of her alive, it circled the drain of that big green tub and slurped its way down to hell.

"What's your book about?" he said softly.

Zelda Fair rolled back in the tub, water breaking over her tummy, rolling down her throat. She called him with one crooked finger and the boy in the silver meringue suit skedaddled over on the quick. She crooked her finger again. He bent down. The reek of gin snaked up his nose—she was swimming in the booze supply. Her pearly dress stuck like an oil slick to her breasts; the drying liquor on her shoulders made her skin prickle.

And then Frankie clued in. From where Zelda was pulling her gin-nymph routine, the acousticals of that pink washroom and the cracked door and the room outside wrestled all together into a weird pool of voices. From where Zelda was bathing, she could hear every word, even whispers, that the party coughed up.

Zelda touched the fennel flower in his buttonhole. She didn't kiss him, though, even though she liked kissing almost as much as talking. Her Mama once said not to kiss anybody you'd told a secret to. It wasn't safe. "If you stick around long enough," she whispered instead, "every night turns into a book. All you gotta do is stick it on a page." A trumpet blurted out something rude in the world outside the pink washroom. "What's yours about?"

Frankie took on a shaky breath. "Things I can't have."

"Mine, too."

1552

NOBODY LIVES IN 1552. Vacancies do happen, even here.

Oh, it won't last. By the party at Robin Hood's pad three flautists from the Philharmonic will have gone in on the place together, pinned up sheet music for wallpaper and liplinered their embouchures with Chanel No. Harlot in the round bathroom mirror. And back around Halloween the short stop for the Yankees called 1552 home and hearth. Poor fella lived in terror of being alone, but got so tongue-tied around the dames that all he could spit out was his own statistics. Miss Georgie knew the shortie plenty well. Every night he called down for Red Riding Hood, Jorinda, Vasilisa, even the odd Momotaro when he felt really out of sorts. It ain't home when it's just the one of me, he explained every time, and home was where he hung his dick.

Folks've done worse to feel safe.

But he got himself traded out to Cleveland and now 1552 has that embarrassed, hangdog look empty flats get, like you seen 'em naked and they don't even know where they lost their clothes to so you're both stuck with looking. This works out for Zelda and her Keychain Knight. Harold Kolburcher can slide that lock as easy as eating. I gotta see, he told Zelda. I gotta see what's on the other side. Won't be a tick.

But there's nothing on the other side. Nothing on the dining room wall where Zelda's closet wall shimmies 1550 up against 1552, where the little sudden door in her closet should open up and say how-do to the ball-player's supper-tray. Smooth, flat drywall, paisley wallpaper, the solid, happy sound of studs where Harold knocks on the wall like somebody in there's gonna answer.

Back over to Zelda Fair sitting cross-legged in her wardrobe, sallow deva floating on a sequin cloud, dresses, both hers and belonging to the O's, thrown everywhere, in baskets, saladbowls, and bunched up on a footstool where she perches, staring at the door in the wall like she's done every day she wasn't fixing stoves since turkey and stuffing ruled the table. Mr. Puss-Boots roosted next to her, balled up tight, his big bill on her knee, half-asleep.

The door's different now. It's gone purple, like it got bruised. There's grapes and oak leaves and seedpods carved on it. The knob is a face with closed eyes.

"It used to be plain white," she whispers when Harold comes back to scratch his bald spot. She starts talking before he's all the way in the room—he jogs to catch up with her talk. "When it got here it was plain white. Brass knob, just a door like every other door in the hotel. I thought: gee, I'm dense! All this time living here and I never noticed there's a door in the closet! But I'm not dense, Mr. K. When we moved in there wasn't anything here but a pelican. I'd've seen it. When I hung up my dresses. When

Ollie hung up her trousers. When Opal stacked up her fabrics in here. We'd all have seen it. There was no door, and then there was a door. That's what happened. And you'd think—wouldn't you think?—when something like that happens it's because it wants you to come in. It wants you inside it. Otherwise why bother? Just kick around Door Park or whatever and mind your own business. But it's locked up good. Doesn't want me, I guess." She reached out her fingers to stroke the door. "Come on, baby. I'm nice. I promise," she whispered. "Everybody says I'm nice." Mr. Puss-Boots chortled softly in his sleep. Zelda never thought pelicans could sound so much like plain old chickens.

"Well, let me at it and we'll see what an old thief can do," Harold sighs.

It's hard going with a pelican staring over your shoulder. It should have been an easy crack. These old skeleton locks, you just look at them sidewise and they cry uncle. But it won't let go. The tumblers won't tumble and the pins won't pin. Sticking his pick in there is like throwing a pencil into a forest. He rubs his neck, sweating fierce.

"Okay, Miss Z, I can bust it off its hinges or I can hack out the lock with a saw. I hate to do it that way. It's brutish and it shows no style. But that's what I got."

"No!" cried Zelda Fair, who can't bear the thought of the door getting hurt on her fault.

"Right. Then I can take a mold and cut a new key for it, and that'll cost you high. But it can't go anywhere, honey. There's nothing on the other end. At best you'd get a little more space for your stockings out of it. I say eat your steaks and pet your bird and go about your life. Like you said. Funny things happen in the world. Probably you were too busy with your hatboxes to notice a little thing like this. Don't you worry about paying me—I didn't do nothing, and nothing deserves no pay. Just you take it easy. Ease up on the drink, maybe."

Exeunt Harold.

Mr. Puss-Boots watches Zelda Fair in her dressing gown, frying her T-bones in an iron skillet. The fat pops; a drop burns the inside of her wrist. The pelican shakes his pouch, which is how his sort says worry. Mr. Puss-Boots loves his girls. They're a damn sight better than the antiques hawker who'd bought him from the Bronx Zoo and pretty much just thought of him as another Chesterfield chair, then fucked off to Mexico and left him with no fish and a dry bathtub. His girls never let the bathtub stand empty. He can paddle about as much as he wanted. And they had herrings all the time.

Zelda tosses him a chunk of beef, which isn't as good as a herring, but what is? She sits in the window while the stars come out, eating her bloody meat, sipping at the silver flask, which turns out to be ginger ale—not the vicious bitter death-causing kind, but ginger ale like it was before ol' Mr. Vollstead ruined everything. Soft and bubbly and sweet and beerily heavy in the blood.

Puss-Boots shuffles his webbed feet. He is a guilty bird. He knows how to get into that door. The key showed its face before the door did. Popped up on the lip of the sink like an old toothbrush. Puss-Boots couldn't help it. It was so shiny. It was so gold and bright. It looked like a herring. It didn't taste like a herring, though. It tasted like a sea with no other pelicans anywhere. He'd kept it at the bottom of his pouch. Didn't want to swallow that night, no sir. Didn't want to give it to Zelda, either. But now she wanted it so bad and he had it and a bird heart can only hold out so long. He wished the O's would come home. They'd drag her out to a party and when Zelda danced she was happier than a basket of eggs.

Mr. Puss-Boots shakes his beak and in another half-second he'd have burped up his secret. But Zelda hops up from the window and makes a beeline for the closet. She has a T-bone in her hand, still stringy with meat and stuffed with marrow. She sits down on the gowns again, holding the bone in her hand like a pistol. It must be the ginger ale moving her hand for her. A girl's hand wouldn't do such a crazy thing.

She sticks the bone in the lock.

And turns it.

And it turns.

The little door in the closet opens inward, all smug and satisfied. Zelda looks down, down down. Down stairs turning circles into the dark.

And then she's gone.

ZELDA LEAVES the door open behind her. When you're that excited, you can't keep silly things like who might follow you on the brain. Mr. Puss-Boots sighs. He bites the door knob and pulls it shut behind him. Humans never clean up after themselves. The pelican takes a deep breath, puffs his feathers like a dandy on a date, opens his wings, and sails out into the great big hulking black space beyond the wall of Room 1552. His wings stretch wide as a diving champion, as wide as he can go, flapping all the way out for the first time since he came to Manhattan. Hot damn it feels good.

It's a long way down.

Part II: COFFIN VARNISH

HOUSEKEEPING

COME ON, DUCKIES. YOU'VE been waiting all this time. I know. I know you. I said there was a basement right there in the beginning and you been waiting for me to get there, drumming your fingers and peeking over the pages for a little peek at something dark. Trying to see round the curtain at my little peep show before I'm ready to show you my big secret Hades-approved hell-titties. Well, hop to it. Put in your dime. Shut the door behind you.

MISS ZELDA Fair, she walks through walls. She walks forever. Forever walks her. Don't seem sensible there should be so much Artemisia in the Artemisia. Her eyes get used to the dark, big as spinning plates. There's blue at the bottom. Blue like water. Blue like an eye.

She thinks on a time when she was just a tiny thing and she found a little cave on the back forty that hadn't been a cave before on account of ferns and mud and mushrooms, but rain washed all that away and left a perfectly marvelous hiding place. Zelda knew it was hers right off. Like a puppy in a shop window. She'd be the Bat-Queen of Slimy Rock and lord it over the Land of the Creepy-Crawlies (which she'd quit being afraid of as soon as possible). She'd dance her ballets in there and be every donna that ever prima'd and the worms would be wowed. They'd applaud all wet and quiet. But Mama Minerva ruined it. Came looking and found little Zelda dressed flash in muck with beetles in her hair. Never again, for goodness sake! Minnie would have it filled in with concrete by supper and Zelda wouldn't have any buttered rolls to boot. Why, Mama?

Because ladies don't crawl into holes, my heavens!

Ladies didn't swim naked either, or smoke or run with boys or cross their legs or curse or eat too much or get blotto because they're bored and only feel half-alive about every other month. Being a lady's just the worst thing since the first thing. Zelda would stay a girl if that was the shape of things, and a girl till she died.

A man's waiting at the bottom of the stairs. Zelda's never met Al before, she don't know him from a cricket. Never been in the basement—too busy upstairs by half. He's all over blue. Blueberry-cream suit with a blue mushroom in his buttonhole, blue light coming out of the pool behind him like the whole sky. His scars look like they could almost spell something, if you could just squint right. Over his shoulder voices whizz and whirr, splashing giggles, the kind of sighing that means somebody's about to get what they want. Thursday is delivery day down here in the underworld and lookie—a surprise package for Al, all wrapped up nice like he likes them.

"Give it over," he says, but he says it with a smile, like he's giving her something.

"What?"

"The nightgown, for starters."

"But then I'll be naked."

"You're already naked, doll."

That doesn't really make any sense, but Zelda strips off her pistachio-green satin sleeping number. Al takes it over his arm.

"Underthings, too, sweetheart."

"But—"

"Price of admission, cupcake! You want in or not?"

"Into what?"

Al grins. It splits his face like another scar. He gestures at her brassiere. Okay, then. Men do always want your underneath, don't they? It's not so odd. Zelda Fair strips down to her belly button. She doesn't even try to cover up with her arms like that stupid Botticelli girl who thought her hair could save her.

"Slippers," he says.

Fine.

"The ribbon in your hair and stop stalling."

Whatever you say, Papa.

Al hands it all off to some tall corpse of a fella Zelda could swear is Mr. Bayeux, the Head Concierge, but she doesn't want to think too long on that.

"Take the third cabana on the left, kitten. I'll be waiting in the shallow end."

Now, probably she shoulda argued, but that man in the blueberry suit didn't even look surprised to see her walk out of the wall, and once you've crawled through a magic door it pays to go with the flow, don't you know? In for a penny and all that jazz.

Red cabana #3 has got a bathing costume for her. Black. Silver stars. A swimming cap with licks of painted blue flames dancing up all over it. When Zelda gets her kit on, she sees underneath it a little china plate from the Green Tabernacle, their own pattern, frogs and treasure boxes dancing round the rim. It's a choice. She knows it right away. Pick one and come on in, the water's fine.

Six red pills. A syringe like a spindle full of woolly moon juice. A matchstick with a thick blue head carved all over with little dancing wooden bodies almost too small to make out their perfect tiny dancing shoes.

Zelda looks at the dish. She thinks about Minerva. About the cave all filled in like a damn pothole.

She takes all three.

B1

EVERYBODY KNOWS A TREE needs water to sink her roots in. The Artemisia gets her end wet in the chlorine paradise under her respectable floors. There's beauty in that pool like chum in the sea. Nobody Zelda recognizes and the It Girl's job description includes knowing everyone and their plus-ones. It looks like one of those flickies where all the girls swim at the same time and turn their heads at the same time and point their toes at the same time while they plunge their heads down under the water like they never needed to breathe in the first place.

Except everybody's kissing. Kissing's like money down below. All you want to do is get some, all anybody wants from you is more. Zelda thinks about blushing good and hard. She's one of those girls born without the natural ability to blush. She had to learn it and Zelda learned by slapping herself whenever she saw something she shouldn't, or felt shamed. Slapped and slapped until her blood knew what to do when the time came. She knew now was a blushing time. So many boys in the water, all perfect and hard and soft and their eyes looked so warm, so warm! Boys laying half in and half out like mermaid, like nymphs, like girls, like Zelda did all the time, lying like you do when you know you're gonna get watched. Lying for someone's lust to land on. And the girls, not lying at all, but hollering and smoking cigars and swigging straight from kegs the size of bedrooms, burping and roaring and telling jokes so raw they sounded like meat. Zelda thinks she's never seen hair shine like it does down there in the pool of wisdom at the bottom of the hotel that was the whole of the world, never seen water bead so perfect on such perfect skin.

Al doesn't indulge. He doesn't sweat in the hot rainstorm funk of the place. The black pillars drip with water, the ceiling glitters wet as starlight. The big man puts out his hand.

"Alberich Mero," goes the chant he's beat out a thousand thousand times, "Huon de Bordeaux, Auboin Charlot, Oberon the Ox of Athens, but you can call me Al, everyone calls me Al, it's easy in the mouth and as true as anything ever is."

She knows who he is, and what she can call him. Everybody knows. Where'd you first hear the name? Beats me. It's written on the walls, brother. Zelda's shy. The nice thing about going to parties and not throwing them is you never have to meet the supply man. You never have to clean up after. Al smells like clover. And beer. And like the cave on the back forty where she danced for the Creepy-Crawlies way back when. But you can't say that stuff to a man with a cut-up face and fists like Judgement Day. You just say something nice, like Zelda did, and this is what Miss Z said, she said:

"You got a lotta names, mister."

"Sure do. I collect 'em. Some fellas like stamps, some go for moths from around the world, but me, I'm the man with the names. Pinned out nice in a case, plucked from the deepest forests this old dumb planet ever dreamed up."

"All I got's Zelda Fair."

"Poor midge. You're only little yet. Maybe if you're good I'll let you borrow one of mine." His piggy eyes go squint. "But you've already been up to borrowing outta my pocket, haven't you? You found my puppy. Naughty thing. Playing with what ain't yours."

"I didn't find any dog! Honest!"

"My door, kid. I keep her on a tight leash, most times, but she does get free on the odd occasion. She loves me brutal. But wild animals gotta hunt. Can't whip it out of them, breed it out, or kiss it out. They'll still trot up to your doorstep, drop a carcass at your feet and expect to be praised."

"I'm not a carcass."

"Everybody's a carcass," Al snaps, and somehow he can snarl and smile at the same time and his teeth look so damn sharp when he does it! Zelda's stomach does a trapeze act. If she could see where the elevator was hiding she'd run to beat the four minute mile. Instead, she talks, because even at the end of the whole world, Zelda Fair could talk the ear off an elephant. She laughs her patented oh-get-over-your-fine-self laugh and bolts on her good-time-girl smile.

"Well, geez, Al, it was just an uppity old laundry chute! I coulda took the elevator if all I wanted was to go down to the basement. You don't have to get fuzzy with me."

Al does the sorta laugh that's not much more than a grown-up grunt. Sounds like a boar rooting in a rock. When he smiles again—Al's smile is the best weapon he owns, better than any pistol or poison, and cheaper on the barrel—his teeth don't look sharp anymore. They look smooth and clean and good, like white cliffs under the moon.

"You're not in the basement," he says.

"Sure I am!"

"No, ma'am. This is the top floor. The penthouse. The show-room show-case show-floor. Why, just look! You can see the whole city from up here."

Zelda looks and sees the boys, she sees the girls, she sees the red silk tents and food like pastel jelly-sherbet-marzipan castles on room service carts the blue water like a chlorinated womb. She sees them swimming at the same time and turning their heads at the same time and pointing their toes at the same time and kissing and sometimes it's boys kissing boys and sometimes it's girls kissing boys but it seems like one way or another this is the place where a boy comes to get kissed. She sees the pills in her hand and the syringe and the matchstick. She sees Al. She sees her face in the pool breaking up into a million squiggly lines. She sees her bare feet, her unpainted toes. She sees the whole city.

"So?" Al coughs. "You wanna see my house? Or you wanna give me back my dog and go upstairs and have some nice milk punch and a shimmy and go to bed at dawn like a good little girl?"

Zelda pulls out her shallowheart gamine-guts I-ain't-nothing-but-a-posy-in-your-pocket laugh. Down here, it sounds like a witch cackling up the toads. Everybody says the basement's Sodom with a Smile On. Once you been there, you can't go home again. You don't even want to. No place for a lady.

Good.

"Gimme the Land of the Creepy-Crawlies," Zelda says, and she says it in her real voice, which decided to show up for work for once. It tastes like bourbon sloshing in her throat.

Al takes her hand all gentle-genteel. Leads her into the water like she's Lillian Gish and there's a new title card going up just as soon as this scene shuts. Al don't get wet. The beautiful boys and the cigar-champing girls open up their arms and Al pulls her down and there's something on the bottom of the pool but she can't see what it is but it might be a mirror and she can see herself in it, the insides of her legs, the insides of her coming up to meet the rest, and he's pulling so hard and Zelda thinks she's gonna drown but she doesn't.

She just sinks.

B2

OH, BABY, IT'S COLD in here. You know that sound outside your window in the wintertime like a bone popping out of its socket, the one your Mama said not to worry about because it's only ice settling? That's the tune on the gramophone now and it never hops a groove. Listen, listen, prick up to the high-hat tsk-tsk-tsk of bare branches against the clouds, the long slow up-against-the-wall of the wind getting down and getting good, the stiff white piano riff of Duke December and his Frostbite Blues.

There's a frozen lake under the Artemisia Hotel. As big as Erie and twice as pissed off. Waves stuck in the middle of crashing, fish clapped up in ice, frozen just as they were about to do a double somersault out of the water and into the sun. Not that there's a sun down here.

A and Z are high-tailing it for the dock. They got a date with that sled there, sitting pretty on this iced cake of a lake in the dark. Hickory wood, curlicue rails, coupla moose ready to pull, black as eighth notes and antlers that could club you to death, lit up candelabra-style, hot fire shooting up from every prong. They are serious moose and no mistaking.

Thursday is delivery day.

Lickety-split and they're off across the great frozen moon-back lake, the moose huffing and the flame spitting and Zelda still in her bathing costume, one giant goosepimple. Al puts a black fur on her shoulders but it's not like when Tommy Germain does it. It's not hers now. It smells like Al and it belongs to Al and when whatever this is quits happening it'll still be Al's. She puts her loot in the pocket anyway, her pills and her needle and her stick.

"Where we going, Al?" she whispers.

"To get the good stuff, buttercup. To see the moonshine, grab onto liquid lightning, hear the hard pop do its hard popping and beat a tune on a barrelhead. Where'd you think booze came from? Can't hit the shops like you used to. No more nice man pulling draughts like a gambler on the slot machines. Asking you how your day's gone. Wiping the countertop like a movie of himself. Can't call up France for a little nip of the good deep red. We gotta go get it. Gotta go to the source."

"Canada?"

Al laughs and his echoes have echoes. The moose scream. Ever heard a moose scream? It's like a pig getting ripped in half.

"Hell yes! Call it Canada if you want. That's a swell name."

And all of the sudden it does smell like Canada, it smells like a border, pine and snow and the exhaust of whiskey trucks waiting on a steel bridge, woodsmoke and spilt gasoline. The mist whips by, tapping out a rhythm on the sled rails.

"Who are you?" Zelda whispers. Her stomach growls but she tells it to shut up.

"I told you. I'm Al. I'm the man with the plan. I came when the liquor dried up—I'm at my best in a wasteland, you know. It's a law, a law of the universe. Like gravity or stupidity or how a minor chord always sounds sad. Take one thing away and another shows up to replace it. Drink is a mighty huge thing to run off with. I'm a mighty huge thing to run to. When I got here, people would sell their own bones for a gulp of something that smelled like a surgeon taking a shit, half wood alcohol, half mold scraped off a rooftop, with a little cyanide and a whack of ginger to give your seizure a nice flavor. What kinda way is that to live? My family, we've had doings with the sauce since before Charlemagne grew a mustache. We put the head on the beer, and we could take it off, too." Al put his hand on his heart. "Oh Lord in Heaven, when I heard my brothers and sisters suffering, travailing, in need, crying out for thirst in this new terrible American desert? What kinda man would I be if I plugged up my ears?"

"Where did you come from?"

"My people are French, if that's your meaning. Had a good old time in England, too. But we don't stick in one place too long. Go where we're needed. Our family crest is a bindle and a toadstool rampant. My man Slake let me set up shop here. He's my kind of drunk: likes the best, turns mean after three drinks, in love with creation after five, and he'll put a bullet in your face without blinking around the time most folks would start throwing up. When I think about it, which is not too often, as I don't waste much oomph trying to get my head around what men have knocking around theirs, I imagine he invited me so this place could get nice and cozy and snail-y. Self-contained, see? If you don't have to go out for booze or food or cunt or cock or even work, you can just carry your house with you. All one. That's what Caspar Slake likes. A cuckoo clock ticking away, little dolls chasing each other round the pendulum, all the parts parting along and no one ever leaves."

Zelda shivers. "And what do you like?"

"Me? Oh, I don't give a fuck about the clock. I like time."

The sled grinds up on the ice-sand shore, crunching and squealing and moosing in the night. There's street lamps on this side. Ice-fishing huts. The dock has a hole in it and it needed new paint a century ago. A little creature comes jumping up to help Al out. He's all rugged up in furs and boots, but Zelda can see his face. Long and blue and pointed, with gold eyes like wedding bands and hair like someone upturned a glass of rum on his head. Cheekbones for miles. He hardly comes up to her waist, but his hands hang down huge, bigger than he could need hands to be, dragging on the frozen beach. He's not a person, not a person like her or the boy who caught her in the bathtub or Oleander Coy or Miss Georgie, but Zelda doesn't want to say so.

"Don't mind my buddy Vollstead." Al booms. "He's my right hand man. Had a vicious row with my old lady over him when he first came to town. Miss T took a shine to him—you never saw anyone so ass-over-the-moon for a mug like his! Good gravy, he looks like someone hit a monkey with a shovel! But if my girl wants something, I want it, too. I want it more than her. I want it harder than her. I want to take it away from her."

"That's a fine way to treat your wife!" cried Zelda.

"I'll thank you to butt out of it! Your kind says I love you all kinds of stupid ways. By punching each other and building railroads and not letting half of you vote and making a million billion more of you and getting old and dying and sometimes by not even being anywhere near the carcass you love. Your crowd's I love you is dumb as rocks if you ask me. So just shut your face about my

I love you. My lady knows what it's all about. Our love is like a sports match. There's rules. There's seventh inning stretches. Sometimes there's bats and a net. She wants something? I get in there first and grab it. I want something? She steals it while I'm sleeping—which is why I don't bother with sleeping. Besides, in this case, I was awfully sweet on him myself. Miss T sat on him for ages, but I got mine. Turned a senator into the spitting image of this old donkey-dicked goblin and off she ran to kiss him dead on the Capitol steps. I do love being married."

Vollstead grins like a kid whose parents got divorced ages ago and it's all rotten but boy, you do get double the birthday presents.. All the earrings in his lace-lettuce ears jingle like saints' days and midnight come at last. He opens his coat like the ghost of Christmas Present only instead of hauling out a couple of Victorian orphans with a lifetime's worth of eyeliner blacked on, he shows his legs: two shiny Tommy guns, their barrels kicking up a lindy. His blue chest is all plastered over with fancy writing like Mr. John Hancock put on the Constitution. He's sporting a beefy-builder's gut, the kind that used to be a wall of muscle, but hey, the championship's not till fall and ice cream's served year round.

"Time to hit the distillery, boss? Yeah? Come on, I'm dying. I ain't walked right for days. My toes is full of bullets and my knees is full of singing!"

"You got it, VS," barks Al. Knuckles that goblin on the chin like a kid off to play ball.

"Al," Zelda says, and her real voice is gone, run off to wherever it hides and licks its wounds every other day but this one. She hates this voice. It's the wheedling, begging voice she learned on her Daddy, the Papa-please-can't-I go-to-the-dance voice, the it's-awfully-cold-mister-say-that's-a-nice-jacket-you-got voice. "Al, I'm starving. Didn't get my eggs this morning. Nor my lunch neither."

"You didn't eat before you got on a moose-sleigh?" Vollstead grimaces, as if he's holding on to a memory of hunger knotted up inside him. "Girl, you gotta be prepared in these parts."

Alberich Mero, the Ox of Athens, shrugs his mighty blueberry shoulders.

"You have food," he snorts, and strides on up the hill through the huts and the lamps and the fog.

"I do not!" Zelda hollers after him. Does the sun ever show its face in Canada? she thinks, even though she knows it isn't Canada really. If nothing else, they speak French in Canada. Mama Minerva and Daddy Rhado took her to Montreal when she was small. She had her first taste of coffee there. She remembers it like her first fuck, and she remembers that plenty well. Al doesn't answer, in French or English or Greek or Scotch-fucking-Gaelic.

Zelda Fair shoves her hands in her furry pockets.

Oh. Oh. She does have food. She closes her hand around the pills. Uppers, downers, lefters, righters? Hell, she's swallowed more mystery medicine than anybody'd care to count at this soiree and that. And what is this but a soiree? She's squired and dressed and got her invitation engraved on a purple door.

Zelda swallows those pills dry. They taste like six warm eggs, like one of Opal's green sequins that she found on her tongue one morning last July, like the pages of a book falling down into her gin-bath like firework wrappers, like Montreal coffee, like a forest in Germany with her name on it, like Miss Georgie's steaks, bloody and scorched at the same time.

B3

THE SUN DOES COME up in Canada. It comes up like a drink at the bar.

Oh, you wouldn't call it a sun. Maybe I wouldn't. But a sun's just a word, you know? A word for whatever makes a body warm and hot and green. What helps a body see past a hand in front of their nose and stretch out nice and wear something other than a whole walrus on their skin to keep from going full ice-cube. What tells the time. The sun in Canada looks like the bottom of an old glass. The light is the color of brandy seeping. It has a taste. Your skin tastes it, like you're all over tongues. The taste is sugar-cane, slowly rotting, turning into the great god rum. It's always that magic hour those film-boys love to shoot down here. Always gold.

And here it comes, that sticky, oily liquor-light, dripping down through trees. Trees! And not frozen, either. Trees of gold and silver and crystal, trees like a table setting, and the winter folds its cards as the lake gets further behind Zelda Fair, turns in its chips, gives up the pot. Leaves roll out; birds cough up springtime and summer close to bursting. She can hear sounds. She knows those sounds. Those sounds are her mother's own voice whispering to a babe at the breast. Those sounds are the joints in her bones. Ragtime plinking, glasses clinking, choruses getting sung with only half the lyrics right, giggles bubbling over like a tower of champagne.

It's a party, shaking down the dawn.

Zelda hobbles up over the hummocky hillocky moor-lumps. She's wearing holes in her feet like a princess dancing too long. No shoes allowed in the swimming pool. No rough-housing. No lifeguard on duty. Her swimming cap still clings to her skull; that black rubber feels like her own skin. It hurts in a funny way. Like she's the purple Hobart and Sons' Fine Smokables sign below their window, the one that lights up Ollie's face every morning like a violet sun as she tells another play to close up its curtains before she comes down there and gives the director a slap in the face. Humming. Hopping. Sizzling around her ears. Boiling, but it's all right because she was meant to boil. Zelda'd take the thing off, but she doesn't know the rules here. What if she needs it later?

And that thing up there? That thing that could be a castle or a villa or a ruin or a chalet or a rack of old dinosaur bones? It's gotta be the distillery. There's barrels like mountains all around it, closing it in, keeping it safe and snug. The taps stick out like proud boys' pricks, bigger than the statues in Union Square, diamond and baleen, gargoyle-spigots tangled up with leaves and berries in their hair. The distillery is a palace without walls. A skeleton of a place. Up rise the arches and struts and buttresses and pillars and load-bearing studs. Up spiral staircases and doorframes to rooms with floors like trellises, floors full of holes and air. Windows float. Doors hinge to nothing. But it's not empty, oh no. There's people milling and swilling everywhere, wearing their Friday best, spangles in every color liquor comes in, black rum and white gin and green abinsthe and pink Hungarian palinka and brown brandy and ginger beer gold. Girls laugh. Their hair giggles down their backs.

Zelda Fair laughs, too. It's parties all the way down.

Only it's not. It's not. Parties are where you go to do nothing as hard as you can. She's past the grand front door now, all frosted glass and brass funny-business, and yes, a man takes her coat, a man with a blue tongue like a lizard, but other than that, reasonably butler-like. And yes, under her coat she's suddenly dressed for a to-do. Her swimming costume has put on airs and swings with glitter-fringe and beads like shotgun pellets. Yes, the sounds bounce and sway just right, yes there is music, yes a smile is a uniform and laughter is a medal of valor—but Zelda's never met a party like this.

Everyone's so awfully busy. A girl dances on a table—and oh! Gee! Zelda knows her! That's Iris Wiltsey, she's Sam Griffith's mistress, the big swinging studio head who comes out from California every month to refresh himself and then straight back to the backlots. Iris is going great guns, moving, her heels striking hard sparks on the slab of table under her. Her red hair flings sweat everywhere. All well and good—but where her feet fall film flickers out, black, shiny ribbons of the stuff, one frame per step, ticking, spooling, piling up around like briars. A man with no shirt on and a chest to write home about pours drinks for his friends at a bar hollowed out of a topaz—why, isn't that Murray Keen, the bellhop with the sweet New England vowels, the one who rooms with Frankie? It is! And when he pours his anise out, it glugs down onto the bar and turns into statues of onyx and marble and bronze, maidens twisted like little Daphnes half-way to turning into sewing machines or clocks or biplanes. Men with triceps to die for crumbling into fennel-flowers, plough-shares, open books.

And there, there's Enzo tucked into a corner with Ollie, Ollie who'd had some boy for weeks and never told, never even squeaked, kissing and grabbing and clinging like they were each a cliff for the other to fall off of. And every time they take a breath, a little slip of a thing escapes their lips, a little gargoyle or medusa or fiery avenging angel or dog-faced carnival boy. Those little thin pictures, well, they drift up like cigarette ash, sticking to whatever they found, turning the bones of the place into confetti colors. And every time he touches her breast or she grabs at his never-you-mind, typewritten columns spiral out, vicious and insightful and clever as death and always utterly right, right for the ages.

Everybody's got something to do but Zelda. Everyone's got the Goods.

"I'm sleeping," she says, and she really believes it just then.

"Nuh-uh," says a little grumble of a voice. She looks down and it's Vollstead standing next to her with a green cigar. "Al is the upside-down man. Back home, you work all day and night to learn how to paint, learn linseed and cadmium and badger-hair and perspective, which is just math in art-school drag, you know? And maybe you still can't do anything worth phoning the Met over. But hey, getting a boy to fuck you is just the easiest thing since Sunday naps. Up top, getting drunk at a party is what you do when you're all out of art. But in…Canada? Are we calling it Canada now? Ok! Al's the King of Canada and he says: fuck that for a lark! The world feels like being a bastard-and-a-half this decade, let's play nine-pins on its grave. Down here it's all the same! Kiss a boy and books come out! Ralph up Parthenons into the upstairs toilet! Dance poems, shit showtunes! Art is easy! Pick up genius at the corner shop! Sell your soul and half your shoes for a glass of gin!" He looks up at Zelda Fair and his poor goblin face goes all twisted up and desperate. "It's all fucked anyway, you see? The end of the world already happened. It's happening all the time. It's gonna happen again. And again after that. Just when you think it's done falling on its face, the world picks itself up and throws itself off a roof. Boom. Pavement. The world's ending forever and ever and we're not even allowed to toast at her funeral. So we gotta do something else or she won't know we ever loved her."

The noise is getting so Zelda can hardly think. Some gramophone somewhere is trilling out a song about how rich daddies never did a girl right since God told Eve she had to clear out her stuff. Vollstead makes a wretched clack-crunch sound and pulls off one of his own legs, hands the tommy gun of his thigh up to her.

"You know what they call one of these in Chicago?"

"I never been to Chicago."

"Al loves that town to death. Me too. Had some of my best days out there. I made that town. Brought her up good." He fingers the barrel of the gun. Zelda thinks he should probably fall over, having only one peg-leg left, but he doesn't. "Anyway, out there they call this baby a typewriter. Get it? Plink-plink-rat-a-tat-smash-punch-carriage-return-bang. Yeah?"

Zelda Fair takes the tommy gun. It's lighter than she thought a gun would be. Feels like a gun should always be heavy like the sun. It's gotta hold all that death. I'm just sleeping, she thinks, and she believes it. When you're sleeping you know how things oughta go, how they fit together. Or maybe you always know but you can't get the rhythm right, and when you're asleep you just go with the beat and the beat don't fail you. So Zelda points the gun at her heart. It's tough. A tommy gun likes to play with others. She has to stick it in the ground and sort of fall over it. But she does. She pulls the trigger with her thumb. That Chicago typewriter rat-a-tat-smash-punches right into her chest.

Pages burst out of the gun, page after page after page, covered with paragraphs, with whole chapters so perfect you could live on them for the rest of your given days. They feel like alive things pushing against her breast, like little animals biting and growling and suckling and baying for meat.

2068

ALL RIGHT, HERE'S THE skinny: it's February and Caspar Slake is fucking Lily Greer in the room next door. There's only four rooms that matter on the 20th floor: the Slake suites, which tumble out like a very nicely upholstered octopus through Rooms 2056-2064, the Valhalla, for visiting how-dos, the Carolingian, for Al's needs when he's up top, and 2068. A few richies take the others when they want to show off, but all the real action's further south on the elevator line, so why put yourself above the fray? Get down where it's at, young man.

So Caspar keeps 2068 nice and plush for his own little frays, his strays, his special ways and means. It's been Lily for three whole months now, and if you're not impressed, you should be. Most don't last three weeks. Lily doesn't live there. Discretion, darling! But it sure is a fine place to spend the night. Done up like a forest in a

French fairy tale, all tapestries and canopies and green glasses full of honey-wine. Not Lily's style, if you asked her about it. Looking up at the scene of a stag getting skewered on the ceiling while a man who could buy the dinky state she was born in bounces up and down on top of her is what a girl might call unsettling. But that's the scene as we come in.

Now, you might think a fella like Caspar is the pits in bed, but he's not half bad. Lily's had worse by a mile. It's been swell, eating fish eggs and angel food cake and peaches from Argentina while lying around naked as a painting. Sometimes he likes her to wear her show costume—she does a regular act down at the Arden Theater as Lily-or-Lyle, the Comic with a Secret! Straps down her tits, slicks her hair, pastes on a mustache with rubber glue, and tells the vaudeville crowds what it's all about. It is currently all about the stupid little blister in her heart where Caspar has rubbed her raw and she hates herself for it but she's started to love him a bit. Lily does not subscribe to love's periodicals. She has a whole set about that at the Arden. How a fella in love isn't a fella at all. Johnny isn't Johnny anymore, he's been replaced by Love, who is not a baby in a diaper but a fat drunk moron who never graduated third grade. Love is nothing but a freak walking around in somebody else's clothes. It's a good bit. Gets them on Lily/Lyle's side. But the point is, you don't love the rich man you're screwing. That's not how the show goes. It's not a good move. Rich men are for fun. That's all they want from you and all you'll get from them, so just sit in it and soak for awhile.

But now she's got a blister on her heart. Like syphilis. She'll have to go see somebody about getting rid of it.

So they fuck on that big green Aquitaine of a bed and it's so good she could eat it for days. She does her Lyle voice for him and he gobbles it up like blackberry pie.

Caspar's just about done fucking her, but she doesn't know it yet. Caspar Slake has a three-month limit at the bar. Any longer and you start thinking about a person different. You start thinking of them like they're yours. You start making plans. He didn't make the rule. It just is. People are clocks who think they wind themselves. Caspar's heard of men who belly about, hollering about how many girls they can stick it in without caring what color eyes they got. But he knows better. Nobody does that. Nobody can. The minute you want somebody more than once, time starts ticking down and all you can do is bug out before the color of their eyes gets to be the only thing in the world that matters at all.

Besides, Pearl always figures out who he's got going by the three-month mark. She's the Hercule Poirot of adultery, that one. Gets out her magnifying glass and peers down the Artemisia, top to bottom. Sometimes Caspar thinks she likes it. It's the flip side of seduction. He chases women, Pearl chases him. He thinks of the pair of them and he thinks of the old German cuckoo clock where Jesus chases Death round and round like a coupla old race-track dogs. She's nearly got Lily in her sights. So that's about that. Maybe he'll see about that girl everyone's talking about on the fifteenth floor, with the giant Gishy eyes and her voice that somehow knows how to blush. Just the voice, none of the rest of her. Caspar likes that. He liked it the first time he met her, when she handed him a bottle still sealed up with blue wax. No label. Liquor colored like squid ink, with little white petals floating at the bottom. Tried to sell it to him for ten bucks. Ten! Her teeth were crooked inside her smile. Been forever since anybody tried to sell Caspar anything as cheap as ten bucks. Been forever since anybody charged him cash money for drink. She didn't have the first foggy notion of who he was. So he paid her. He kissed her. She let him, maybe even kissed him back, though when he got his arm around her waist and crushed her up to him a little, she laughed like he'd made the best joke since the first man walked into the first bar. Said her name was Zelda and there was more where that came from and hopped away. Yeah, he might have to ask after that one. She had ankles that looked like they'd shatter if you pinched them. Or maybe he'd just call down to Georgie and have her send up a Rapunzel or two.

Here's a pair of things Caspar doesn't know yet. Just to get a good punch in for Lily. Right about the time he's doing his best thing in her and turning red and thinking of Zelda's crooked teeth and shutting his eyes and crying out all desperate and sincere like humans love to do, just about that time, when he's decided to take Lily's pretty silver 2068 key back this very night, Caspar Slake is fixing his death in place, just as neat as a nail for a picture that ain't been bought yet.

And Pearl de Acosti y Candela y Slake?

Oh, she's gone.

1633

IT'S NOT JUST PEARL, oh no. The Artemisia's got a hole in her pocket. She's lost a whole batch of things down there. Lint, quarters, cigarettes, buttons, hairpins, Pearl Slake, Oleander Coy, Murray Keen, Olive Bay, Enzo Bacchi, Dandy Brute, Iris Wiltsey, Ogedei the Mongolian eagle, car keys, breath mints, Lily Greer, lipstick, a pair of Texas twins name of Nickel and Dime. A pelican.

Zelda Fair.

For once, folk notice when Zelda runs off. This is because Zelda, of late, has had the good stuff. Her black booze got you so drunk you thought your name was William. And if your name was William, you'd swear it was Nebuchadnezzar, King of the Buffalo. Zelda's shit is the best shit this side of Shit-City. I heard a girlie got ahold of a whole bottle to herself—and how she pulled that off I couldn't tell you. Miss Z started out at ten smackers, but inside a week she was up to fifty per, and yesterday I couldn't get one for seventy-five. Anyway, this little bitsy thing, circus girl, top of the trapeze pyramid or something, couldn't weigh more than my little finger, got a whole bottle of Zelda's medicine and hogged it all. Drank and drank. Told everybody she was gonna find the perfect mixer for this growler whiskey right here. Drank it with tonic, drank it with orange juice, apple juice, grapefruit, tomato, drank it with ginger ale, drank it with Coke, drank it with bitters and champagne, drank it with lemonade. By the end she was drinking it with tears and calling poor Mad Mauler Morrison the Lord of the Moon. She dubbed that nice boy who writes obituaries for the Times Ganymede, Jupiter's Slave, and insisted that she was the new Christ, Star of the West, anointed with gin, and she came to bring not the sword but the juniper branch, and where there was one blue bottle of Bombay Sapphire and one fried potato she would make a wedding feast of five thousand Queen Victorias and five thousand chips with vinegar and then she didn't wake up for a week. When she did wake up, she went into mourning for her husband, Stone Boy, who was eaten by a lion. Wore black. Whipped her back raw with her circus buddy's crack-whip. Cried like the world went and broke. Thing is, she'd never been married in her life. Barely a kid herself.

Zelda's shit is the only shit.

She sells it out of thigh-holsters like a gunslinger. Ask her for liquor and she opens her legs, pulls out heaven, and charges you way too much for the privilege but you don't even mind. She'd show up to a party, giggle and dance and tell the one about the guy on 42nd St with the hippo in his handbag, sell out her stock, and pass out asleep under the dining table. After 10 pm, every party played Find Zelda. So when suddenly there's no holsters and no black bottles of white petals and no new Christs vomiting in the bathroom, everybody notices.

Josie Shadduck loses his damn mind. Puts reward sheets up in the elevators like he's living in the Old West. Threatens anybody he thinks so much as smells like her. Starts carrying around a flickie-knife so he can keep to a tight schedule of screaming and brandishing. The things he accuses those boys of you never heard in all your days! Fuck-and-kill combos not even that Ripper fella in London could dream up. What did you do to my wife? Tell me! And God in his heavenly hammock help you if you point out that Josie wasn't even the least littlest bit married to her. Which is where he crosses Tommy Germain, who wanders around the halls like a Gothic gentleman, wailing and weeping about his wife, which Zelda was also not, and it's a little known fact I don't mind sharing that eventually Josiah Shadduck III stabbed Thomas Wyclyffe Germain outside Room 1633 for sniffling over how much he missed his dear, beloved, precious wifey-poo.

Oh, calm down. Josie got him in the love-handle. Germain dropped like a cartoon anvil but it wasn't much of anything but funny. The joke comes out best when you consider those two made a bouncing baby electricity company together about ten years later, and they're probably the fellas keeping the light on while you read right this very instant.

William Hessen-Hyde hoards. Hoards all the bottles he could get off of anyone. Buys, steals, grabs, swaps. Even a half-drunk bottle. Even a snifter with a little left at the bottom. Hoards it all up in his room till he's surrounded by glasses full of black booze like church candles. He doesn't call Zelda his wife. He doesn't promise a million bucks to the guy who brings her home. He just sits seething in the middle of all that bum-rum, snorting through his nose like a boar. And then he starts drinking.

So Zelda's skedaddled. Sure. Okay.

But when Pearl pops off, all hell breaks loose.

288

SEE FRANTIC FRANKIE DO the Lost Girl Rag!

He doesn't hear the news till everyone else already knows. See, Frankie doesn't get invited to the good parties. He's never even tasted that hellcat hooch Murray's always on about. Murray comes home at end of shift wearing his rowing crew New England ivy-up-his-ass looks. Looks like that irritate Frankie. They don't mean anything. They're as good as a $50 tie and they come for free. Anyhow, Murray comes home with a little nip in his pocket one night, a nip of something new. He's barely nabbed more than a damn test tube of the stuff, but he doesn't share. Murray sits in the window nook and slurps down his loot and after awhile he starts talking to the fire escape. Tells it all his secrets. Calls it Mathilda. Tells it he loves it, his rust iron golem princess, and when he's saved up enough he'll take Mattie away from this awful place. When he's made a man of himself.

They'll go out west together. Maybe Iowa. Have babies with rungs so strong you could hang all your faith on them and they'd never bend. If she'll just let him have his way this once. Frankie stops feeling quite so hung up on Murray's $50 pinstriped face.

But Room 212, she's getting pretty empty these days. Frankie never sees his roommates anymore. Everyone's busy, he supposes. Everyone's got a sweetheart somewhere. He lays about the room like the kind of guy who doesn't need to split the rent. It's nice. He looks at Enzo's drawings under the windowsill. A satyr is licking the ledge. He's got a fawn in each hand, and the fawns have girl-faces. The same girl face, which Frankie never noticed before now. Oleander Coy's face, with the quirk in her jaw that says go ahead, impress me. I've got all night. Huh, Frankie thinks. Would you look at that.

Frankie still reads the news through the tubes. Copies it out before his poor brain can chew it soft enough to swallow. So he reads it in his own hand, like he did it, like he made it happen.

Zelda's bugged out. Haven't seen her in a week. No more black punch. Think she went to Canada. —Ollie, Room 1550

Frankie's stomach drops down to his shoes. His hands sweat. Canada? What does a girl like that want with Canada? Then his thoughts wriggle out of his head, crazy on panic and gin-shakes. Did he have enough money to head up there? Probably not. Montreal's closest—but maybe she didn't speak French. Don't be stupid, of course she speaks French.

Frankie saw Zelda just once after the bathtub. She came to 212 and knocked like she didn't really know how. He'd answered in his pajamas, a little striped number like you see in the pictures. She looked at him with big old circles under her eyes like a raccoon in the daytime, like she didn't expect herself to be where she was, and maybe didn't even know where that might be. She just stood there in the hall in a bathing suit, but she wasn't wet. Shivering, but not wet. Stood in the hall in a bathing suit and opened her mouth and closed it and perched sort of on one leg like one of those goofy flamingoes.

"Zelda?" He'd asked.

"Yeah?" she whispered.

"What...can I do something for you?"

She stared at him, just so confused, like he'd asked her to dinner in Hungarian.

"I thought you wanted me."

And she ran off. Like she was running from his wanting. He didn't run after her, more fool him, and if you asked, he couldn't tell you why, why not then, when in just a minute he's going to run after her harder than a hunting dog.

FRANKIE KEY gets called into Room 288. It's where Raspail Bayeux, the Head Concierge, makes his digs. But Raspy isn't alone behind his big old warship of a desk, with its green lamp glowing at one end like the light at the end of a dock. Caspar Slake is there, the man up top, the guy who owns the whole shebang. Frankie's never seen him before. The cat's not as old as he figured. Wears his clothes like he was born in a three-piece suit.

"I have a job for you, Francis," Raspy says in the voice he uses to direct guests to one restaurant over another. The paprikash at the Blue Heart Cafe is particularly good today, sir. "There will be good compensation, both financial and otherwise. If you're interested."

Caspar Slake gives him the up-and-down. "My wife's gone missing," he growls, like Frankie did it, somehow, and did it on purpose.

Frankie's written this kind of thing a hundred times. He twigs to the situation double quick.

"I'm no detective, sir," he hurries.

"You kids all know each other," Caspar hisses. He hasn't slept in a dog's age. Eyes all red like his eyeballs could smoke the cigarettes themselves. He's put holes in the wall on six floors with his fists. Little Cass is hiding in the libraries on seventeen, at least, Big Cass thinks so. He's got bigger problems than his boy. But Little Cass isn't there anymore, only his daddy doesn't know it yet. "You all cover for each other. You must know. If one of you knows, you all know."

"She's not the only one," Mr. Bayeux says quietly.

"She's the only one that matters!" Slake snaps.

"Of course, sir." Might I recommend the lobster at the Silver Umbrella? Frankie wonders if Raspy ever stops using that voice. If he even has another one. Raspy pushes a sheet of paper across the bow of his desk.

"This is a list. You don't have to tell us anything right now. If you get results, they won't be questioned."

Frankie looks at the names. All those dancing princesses, skipping the hop down to the underground.

"But don't know anything. Believe me. I work, that's all I do. If not on the floor, on my books. Nobody tells me anything. I'm a terrible person for the job, honestly. Just about anyone else would be more tuned in than me. I mean, have you asked Al? I'd ask Al. I just write detective stories. When people go missing in real life they're usually...well, usually dead. And when people go dead, usually you never find out why."

Raspy and Caspar glance at each other. They'd ask Al if they could. But you don't ring-a-ding and summon the guy like a bellhop.

"She might be up on 201st Street for all I know. Or New Jersey. Or France. It's impossible." Frankie's starting to panic. Sure, it's nice to have a rich man grateful to you, but it's miserable to fall down on the job he hands you.

Everybody's real quiet. The kind of quiet that's both the asking and the answering. She's not in France or New Jersey or up in the nosebleeds. Frankie doesn't know much but he knows a little. Raspy and Caspy know a lot more. There's no world outside the hotel once you've lived here long enough, and Miss Pearl's lived there from day one. She's here. And even if you don't know where the good gin's pouring on any given night, you know where people go when they disappear in the Artemisia. And if Zelda went to Canada, Frankie knows he's staying Stateside.

"Why me?" he croaks.

Raspy has a little chuckle. "Well, my lad, between the mad, the drunk, the psychotic, and the consumptive, you're the only one left."

Part III:

SODA POP MOON

LOBBY

IT'S NOT HARD TO begin. It isn't ever hard to start—not stories, not jobs, not flings. It's the finishing that sticks in your jaw. Frankie always liked starting a story best. Putting a hat on his detective, grey or white or black or buff or blue. Deciding who's dead. Deciding who wants them not to be dead. Putting shops on the street where Hank Hart or Ken Sharp or Walter Bent keeps his office. Good old Wally. Does he like bourbon or opium? Is he a teetotaler? Will he survive the story? It's good to live in the beginning. In the Not-Yet, like Zelda said. So right now, Frankie is all right. He hasn't screwed up yet. He hasn't rushed the ending or blown out the plot like a flabby tire. He has a place to go, first off. He hasn't got a hat, but he's got a mysterious girl love interest and one pair of good shoes and that's a start. He's worked with way less than that.

Frankie goes to the only secret place he knows in the Artemisia. It's where he gets his paychecks. A little room in the lobby, past the fountain full of gargling seals and their balls all covered with stars, past the soda fountain and the concierge desk and the check-in counter, between the Silver Umbrella restaurant (French and Continental) and the Blue Heart Cafe (Hungarian). It's a wall and it's a door and it's nothing at all. It's magic, Frankie knows that, even if he doesn't like to say that word, even if that word is almost like a swear word around here, falls flatter and harder than an uncareful fuck or cunt at the supper table. But he still thinks it's the kind of magic fellas down on 42nd St do up on stage in tuxedos, the kind that goes abracadabra and then there's a bunny.

Here's the bunny.

If you stand in front of the paisley wallpaper, right where the blue swirls look like eyes and the oak leafing looks like scrambled green eggs, between the two cafes, and order a croque monsieur with extra gruyere and boysenberry jam, pretty soon after there'll be a silver dish with a check on it waiting for you in the service elevator, sitting fine as you like on the operator's plush stool. The dish always beats you to the elevator, even if you take off at a dead run halfway through the -yere in gruyere. It does this time, too. Frankie's sopping when he rips the gate open, sweating like he gets paid by the drop. But it's not a check, no sir.

It's a swimming cap. Black with silver stars.

And a little card with some awful nice handwriting on it. The handwriting says Midnight. The Ballroom.

THING IS, Al won't close the door on anyone. His parties have room for all. Come on in. Nobody to look at you funny in here. Nobody to tell you not to have that drink, kiss that fella, smash that chair, light that chandelier on fire. Do it all. Do it forever. It's not Al's style to wall up his best so a boy like Frankie can't get at it. He doesn't dance to that jig. The more the merrier, and Al is all about making merry. Brick by brick, hinge by hinge. Al loves you, kids. From the bottom of your bones.

Trouble with love is it wants company.

BANQUET HALL

AL CAME INTO THIS world dancing shoes first, and that's the way he'll go out, if he ever does go out. But really, kittens, what are the chances of that? You could say a dance is all he is. Used to be nothing much to do in this world but eating, fucking, killing, trying not to get killed, having babies, and, if your particular local glaciers weren't too much of a drag, picking berries off the bush and apples from the tree. Back then, Al and his people were a little like dinosaurs. They were bigger than us and better fixed for this world. Sharper teeth, quicker on their feet, lighter bones. Muscles like funny tight braids. They could see better in the dark. Had a couple of different brains to handle the extra load. Larynxes that could make noises that weren't vowels or consonants but something else, something that could glottal-trot and whistle-waltz so that only wolves and dragonflies could hear. Sometimes they had tails. Sometimes horns.

They'd been around for a dog's age, going about the good animal life, laying eggs, guarding nests, sucking marrow, writing poems on buttercup stems.

They worried a bit when we figured out fire. Watched us watching it, watching it like it was holy, like it was gonna save us from something, which is all holy's ever meant. They didn't like how we watched our fire. See, not a one of Al's folk ever had to suss out how to make things burn. Or build a hut or chase a mammoth off a cliff or knap a knife or blow through a hollow sheep-bone to make a song or cut a hunk of fur into a person-shape to keep warm when the stars go winter. They've got all that inside them. Like you and I got livers. We don't have to think about how our liver works, it just does its thing and all's well. One of them could look at a mammoth and it'd find its own cliff and taking a flying leap without so much as a sure, boss. They were knives and fur and songs and burning, they burned all the time, so hot it hurt their bellies, but they couldn't help it, they crackled and forked and from a ways away it always did look like sparkling.

So there we were, eating and fucking and killing and trying not to get killed and picking berries and munching apples and lighting sticks against the dark. I just felt sorry for the poor bastards, Al says when you ask him about it, which you should, if your brain is tired of thinking in just the one direction. Anybody gives their dogs toys, don't they? You don't just let them lie around in their own shit getting so bored they tear up the sofa just to get a little attention. They were just so cute and helpless. I've always had a soft heart.

So up comes Al and he says to some sad sack of cavemen wearing bear feet over their people feet 'cause the stink is a damn sight better than ten toes worth of frostbite and he says:

"Hey, cats and kittens, lambs and rams, ladies and gents! Have I got something for you! One hundred percent brand spanking new! You'll love it, I promise. It'll knock you flat. It'll make you feel like a million bucks. What's a buck? Oh, bucks are fun, you'll find out later. But what I got? It'll make a new man out of you. You'll wanna tell all your friends. It'll fix you up if you're sick and make you grin if you're grim. And it won't cost a thing. Just take this patch of mammoth butt and stretch it out over these branches, nice and tight, yeah? Tighter than that, even. Come on, put your back into it! There you go! Then you take your hand and you whack it. Whack it again. Whack it quick and whack it slow. Whack it three times, hold still for a sec, then three more times. Two, then three, then four, then hold up, hold up—then five as quick as you can. That's it, any way you want, loud as you can stand it. Look at you, little drummer girl! Pa-rum-pa-rum-pum! Now just do like I do."

That's what Al does. That's what he asks. Just do like I do. Be like I am. Faster, quicker, harder, hold still, do it again.

He showed them how to lift up their people-feet-inside-bear-feet and put them down again on the beat. How to shake their hands and shimmy their hips and do a little soft-shoe on the roof of their caves. He taught them so good they couldn't stop. It was more fun than staring at fire.

But Al couldn't stop either.

"Hey, man, how about you rip up that cat with the fluffy tail? If you dry out his guts and twist them up real good you can strum something better than drumming. Don't worry, that cat probably don't mind. Being music is a damn sight better than being a cat. If you put holes in his bones and blow your breath through his death, you can make just the sweetest sound you ever heard. And hoo boy, lookee here, if you eat these berries instead of those, you'll see stars. Stars like being born! Come on now, eat up, there's a good ape. Now, I know you won't believe me! But if you leave this particular sort of green fuzzy grass in a bunch of water for a spell, it'll turn into beer. What's beer? Why, kid, beer's your best friend. And if you think dancing to dead cat and mammoth ass is good now, just you wait till beer cuts in and shows you how to do-si-do. Aw, look at you. You drew a horsey on the wall! Aren't you clever. Com'ere and let old Uncle Al give you a kiss."

And that's how people learned to dance. For a good spit of the world, we danced with Al's crowd and everything was fine as fairy-dust. Sometimes us and them liked the look of each other and it wasn't easy, but where there's a lust, there's a way. Sometimes we got afraid that they'd take it all away. The dancing and the music and the beer and the dead cats that somehow made us cry when you rubbed horse hair against their guts and we'd have to go back to being entertained by the rot of bear feet on our real feet. So then we killed some of them and they killed some of us. But there was always more of us. Life is a numbers racket. They lived a lot longer, but we made more, made them faster, and made them in style. Al did all right with the dancing, the rest of his people said, but maybe he should have cooled it with the beer.

And I know you won't believe me, but it's dancing that made everything else. Once we get ahold of something, we want more and we want it now. More music, more liquor, more dancing, and to get those things and keep those things, you gotta plant things in the ground, try your breath on the bones of every thing that has them, remember the best songs and figure out how to write them down so when somebody's blowing on your bones, the songs keep on. To have a really good party, you gotta make some swell houses, light them up, paint the walls, invent tables so you can dance on top of them, and doesn't all that booze taste nice cold?

We got busy. We called those old dinosaurs God for awhile.

Then the Devil. Then cute little chorus girls with nice gams in plays about dreams. They didn't go away. They just weren't first on the guest list anymore. And still, Al couldn't ever leave us be. Why should he? He'll tell you for free. If you feed something long enough, you own it. He just keeps on shoveling music and dancing and death and blood and his best hooch onto our plates. He'd tell you he's been pretty damn honest all along. Music is made out of death. Mammoths and horses and cats all in cairns and that's how you get Mozart and Euripides and Fats Waller. Dancing is a funeral, too, waltzing down the elephants you killed so you and yours could have one more night when you could forget that the glaciers are still at the door, that there's still nothing but eating and fucking and killing and trying not to get killed and berries that make you see stars and apples that make you see the difference between what's good and what's bad.

You always trade blood for joy. It's always a deal struck in the wet and the dark. Al didn't make the rules. He just dances to the song that's playing. He wants things, too. And I asked him once but he didn't say, so I'm just going to tell you what I think. That's cool, right?

I think Al just wants to feel like he did that first night he showed a caveman how to make a drum and thump the ground. Wants to be the whole world waiting to happen to somebody. Wants to look at a person and see civilization spin up in their eyes, but not just civilization, not just thousands of years of dancing, dancing on pyramids, dancing on galleons, dancing on rockets, dancing on Arcturus, not just that, but also love like pyramids and galleons and rockets. Love like being born. The kind of love you give a guy who taught you everything you know. Everything that matters.

Even if he's a son of a bitch.

THE GRAND BALLROOM

SO FRANKIE KEY, HE walks into the Grand Ballroom. And people there are doing what they've always done. Slake rolled out fake grass over the floor last summer so folks could practice their putting. Thousands of strands of silk and wool and satin. Looks like the real thing. Even smells like it—some perfumer in the Financial District whipped up a batch of 9th Hole Ambrosia: good soil and sprinkler water and fresh, dewy blades of grass with a little hot hazard sand and moist pond water sliced in for good measure. Green as England. And everyone's barefoot on this grass that isn't grass, dancing quick and slow, quick and slow, quick, quick, slow, slow. A couple of old-timers are playing through some infinite eighteenth hole, sinking balls like pearls into black mouths in the floor. A bunch of girls with violets in their hair play croquet, whacking their mallets so hard the balls sail over the dancers, through their swinging, waving arms. A red one shatters a wall-lamp. Everyone laughs. Music plays through, too, mammoth music, cat music, horse music, from five pianos, ten guitars, about a hundred drums, a couple of horns and maybe a squeezebox, and they're all playing different songs, different times, different everything, but somehow it's not and they're all together, the piano boys and the horn-girls and the drummers everywhere and the strummers, too, and the squeezebox orphan squeezing like she's gonna die any minute and this is the last polka she's got.

And Frankie walks through it all like somebody's dad. Nobody meets his eye. Backs get turned one by one, bare and glittered and tuxed and tailed. Champagne conversation bubbles and foams and bubbles down to the floor and not one gulp of it goes hey buddy where'd you come from? Can I get you a canape? Sippa somethin' nice? No girl dancing by her lonesome looks up with hope when Frankie's shadow hits her shoes. No boy brushes up against him in that way that feels like a sweet, soft, uncertain question. He's nothing. He's no one. He's invisible.

Frankie's a fella who likes his books, so he thinks of Perseus. He thinks of the cap of darkness that slick got on his way to look at an ugly dame. Thinks of Andromeda, tied up to a rock waiting for a whale to show her into his guts. He walks by a tap-dancing boy with suspenders chippered up with sapphires and white bows and a chin you coulda ordered from a catalogue. The boy taps on Frankie's big toe and just keeps on going. Frankie yelps. The boy doesn't even glance. Three girls who work together selling cigarettes and candy at the cinema down on 44th pass a silver compact between them, each taking their turn looking in the glass before passing it on like a joint, like a flask, like a sacred, all-seeing, all-judging eye. He tips his hat. They don't blink. Maybe it's Al's magic, making him scarce. Maybe it's the swimming cap he's got stuffed in his pocket like a showgirl's panties.

Nah.

It's a simpler magic. An older magic. Older than Perseus? You bet. Older than Father Time's greatest hits. Rich man's magic, and here it is:

Nobody minds the help.

Frankie's in his bellhop glad rags, brass buttons and bombazine twill and a pillbox cap of green, green darkness with a chinstrap so it stays on even if he should happen to need to go on hands and knees in the dumpster out back for some four-year-old princess's favorite blue ribbon. Nobody wants to lock eyes with the guy who's gonna have to clean up their good time while they sleep it off. Nobody's looking to go home with the staff at midnight—that action only starts around three in the a.m., when other choices have split. I'll tell you what, Perseus never had it so good. Mr. P was a god's son, which is just another way of saying old money. Everywhere that cat went people gave him their best goat. He had the shiniest hair and the best teeth. But he needed magic to get ignored by the world. Magic knitted in hell by a chick with three faces and a mean backhand.

Frankie can do that shit for free.

He just slips on by. It shakes him up at first. Even a bellhop, when he's a nice-looking white boy with a degree in one pocket and his mother's love in the other, wants to be seen. Likes to be seen. Hell, doesn't everyone? But Frankie's always been seen. He's used to it. He likes it. Likes how folks ask the time on the street because they know a chap like him has a watch. Likes how he gets to say who he wants for President in a bar and everyone nods agreement. Likes how his name sits on a magazine cover, his own honest-born name, even if it's in tiny yellow print at the bottom corner under an ad for detergent. Even in his Artemisia get-up, when he goes to somebody's door, he's expected. They shake his hand, tip him for his trouble. Call him a nice young man. But now, when the party's sprawled over the fake grass, wine glasses sunk in the golf-green, bubbly holes-in-one, when he should be glowing like a dock light, he's a ghost.

The writer in him, though, the writer in him likes it fine. He can listen like a mouse at a cat congress. It's almost like manning the tubes. Coy never came to my show. Never wrote a word about it. We had to close inside a week. What can you do? Come on baby, the wife's in Spain. I've got my money in rail, mostly, but I'm branching out into pharmaceuticals. Sounds grand, mister. Got anymore of that black-bottle stuff? Opium never got me so high…

And just like that he's bored. It's not like the tubes, it's just the same. There's no such thing as a secret, really. The only secret is: I want something I don't have. I'm dying for it. Losing sleep. Give it, Christ, give it here or I don't know what I'll do. And sometimes it's something they shouldn't have and sometimes it's something they'll never have and sometimes it's peace of mind and sometimes it's the end to all wars but mostly it's just money or love. Money or love. Money that looks like love and love that looks like money. And since Frankie's dying for those, too, he's bored by them, by everyone else panting after them just like him.

He tries talking.

Al sent me: to an elderly golfer with plaid pants and pound coins in his loafers. Have you seen Al tonight: to a dowager wearing three ivory black-backed cameos. Can you get into the basement from here: to the piano-player with marigolds braided in his black beard, who brought his music downtown even though it's the only precious thing he's got and these dumb white drunks just eat it without tasting.

Nobody answers. They look past him. They don't see. They shift a glass from one hand to another, tap a ball like a bank safe and send it to its final resting place, shift the song into G Major and sing out: send this orphan boy home, home, home before he ain't got nothing left but his bones, bones, bones. Frankie can't figure it out. Al's always been there with a pun and a paycheck whenever they've met. What's he done wrong?

Okay, he tells himself, you're a gumshoe. You're Frankie K. Frankie the Ghost. Strong and silent. On the case. What are your assets? He pats his chest, his front pockets, his back pockets, the atheist's genuflection. Billfold, skeleton key, notepad, pen. Safety pin. Hard cherry candy.

Swimming cap.

Frankie the Ghost yanks off his pillbox bellhop crown and stretches the black shiny latex over his hair, ripping out strands of his straw-colored mop-top. Silver stars pop into place over his ears. He fits the rubber chinstrap nice and tight.

And falls to the ground. To the fake grass. To the green.

Agony arcs through his skull, electric firework horror ticker tape flick-film. His eyes bulge, muscles lock up, spine turns to a pillar of sizzling salt. An heiress steps over him, losing her slingback as she goes, sticking its cream leather heel in his back pocket. She scuttles for the bar rather than go back for it and have to make little puppy noises like she cares. Frankie tries to get his hands up under the cap to get it off, get it off, but his elbows are frozen in pain like a stuck bomb, halfway blown. He's making a scene, now. His invisibility won't hold much longer. Poor lamb.

The cat in the plaid pants comes up behind him. Trying to play through, just like the rest of us. He winds back his putter like St. So-and-So's lance and knocks Frankie in the rear. It's not a tough shot. The old codger will make par in the ballroom, that's for sure. And even though he doesn't want to, doesn't even seem like that knock should do a damn thing, Frankie rolls. He rolls toward the golf hole with a proud 18 flag and a broken champagne flute sticking out of it. It's black in there, blacker than it should be, and bigger than it should be, and he's teetering toward it, electric night still rutting his brain into obliteration, and it opens like a sinkhole, like quicksand, like the doors to the Artemisia, like money and love and Zelda in the bathtub, it opens like a book waiting to be written, and Frankie the Ghost is falling under grass.

B2

HATCHA GOT THAT ON for?”

It’s a voice he knows. A silly, laughing voice. A voice out of a schoolyard, teasing, coaxing, the kind of voice that invites you back behind the gymnasium for one glorious cigarette, shared like communion, transubstantiated into the holiest of nicotine-spirits by her hand.

It’s Zelda.

The first face you see in the underworld is always the one you want most. It’s like that first hit of morphine—free of charge, baby. Just a taste.

“You can see me,” Frankie gasps.

“’Course I can, silly. I got 20/a million peepers these days. And I see you got something that’s mine,” Zelda says, and pulls the swimming cap off him, the chinstrap dangling free in her hand like a black noose. "You can't have it."

Frankie's jaw unlocks. His brain starts to soften back into the good goo of grey and pink and thinking. His bones quit doing their poison puppet act. He gets on with breathing and every time he manages it it's less like choking on sour fire. He looks up and she's there, bending over him, fastening the cap on her own head. She just looks at him, not even really smiling, but almost halfway to the county where smiling lives. Rubs her arms in the chill. Everything smells like pine and ice and starlight. Did you know starlight has a smell? Well, at least it does in Canada. Smells like vodka and lime and a splash of bitters, hand to God.

"Doesn't that hurt?" Frankie coughs. His spit freezes when it hits the ground.

"What doesn't? But some kinds of hurt almost feel good, you know? Familiar. Like an ugly couch in your parents house with the springs all bare where your daddy slapped you once for coming home late and now when you sleep on it it's like one of those Indian fellas napping on nails but it makes you feel like you come from somewhere. Hurts like home. I always wear this when I'm down here. How'd you get it?"

"I found it."

And Zelda shrugs like it doesn't matter. She looks up and off over a rise full of frozen real grass, not perfect silk golf grass, grass with big beardy crusts of cold all over. They're on a lakeshore, Frankie realizes. A lakeshore in winter and even the sand is half ice. Zelda's wearing fur, a black fur coat like a senator's mistress only it's hers, it's so clearly hers, she's so at home in it she looks naked even though he can only see the pale punctuation of her face at the top of the ruff. She doesn't look like he remembers her, like the dog-eared faded bathtub memory he keeps under his heart. Frankie has a mad thought—she looks like architecture. Like some permanent, chiseled thing so deliberate and designed and lovingly hacked out of stone that tourists come to look at it and wish they lived somewhere they could look out of their kitchen window and see just one corner of it every day. She looks like one of Al's people. Oh, not like Frankie. Not like Al's errand boys and good time girls. One of his people. One of the odd ducks off in the shadows in long coats and long dresses and eyes that don't shine in the dark, one of the ones always writing or counting or checking the time while Al does his softshoe workin'-for-me's-like-working-for-springtime come hither pitch.

"Zelda, where have you been? What are you doing down here?"

Her eyes slip back toward his.

"Working," she says, and her voice is so full of thrill at that word Frankie is sure she said something else for a minute. Winning, maybe, or wanting. "Come on, I'll show you."

She hauls him up the winter dunes. He turns up the collar on his bellhop uniform. The sky overhead is so clotted with stars, like they're all in a hurry to get somewhere. To get here. Zelda walks like this is her own backyard, and pretty soon she's gonna show him a rope swing she was too afraid to try till she was thirteen.

"Have you ever been to Canada before?" Zelda says instead. She's different—less interested in him. Frankie hates it.

"No ma'am," he starts to say before he understands that she don't mean any place whose capital is Ottawa. But the answer is still no. "I just work for Al, up top. Keeping...keeping books." He finds he doesn't really want to say anything about the tubes. She might think it was wrong, that he'd seen things he shouldn't, which of course he has. "I asked once. If I could see the basement. Always heard the parties there were like something out of the

Bible. The good parts of the Bible, before God gets mad and raids the place. But he said it wasn't for me. Not for a nice Minnesota boy with milk for blood. I insisted and he said…" Frankie winces. He remembers every word. "He said I'd just blab it all to everyone because that's what good schoolboys who grow up writers do, and maybe when I was forty and had drunk down a dozen movies and saw despair in my own buttonholes, then I could be trusted." Zelda doesn't laugh at him. That's something. "Do you like it here?" he ventures, pressing his luck.

"It's the best place in the world," she says, and she means it, he thinks, more than he's ever heard anyone mean a thing. He's jealous of this place all the sudden, she means it so hard. "So how come you're here now, if he blew you off?"

"I'm…I'm looking for someone."

The schoolyard cigarette voice clicks back on like a light. "For me? That's awfully sweet."

"No," he says, and feels sick because of course it's her, who else but her? "For Pearl Slake. Y Candywhatever. I'm supposed to bring her home. Have you seen her?"

"Well, sure."

"Is she well?"

"So well you could throw pennies in her. But I don't think she'll want to go home. I wouldn't mention it, if I were you. She throws things when she's mad."

A grand set of mountains brushes up against the stars far ahead. Frankie can see a house—but you couldn't all it a house. It's huge, bigger than a castle, bigger than he imagines Versailles could ever hope to grow up to be. It has no walls. It's bones against the dark. Glowing, glittering bones, ringed in by barrels like Greek temples. He tugs Zelda's furry arm back. Before they get there, he has to ask. He has to know.

"Zelda, Zelda, wait. Wait." She looks at him with a perfectly open, sunny face, the swimming cap that hurt him so covering her ears snug and cozy. "Do you like me?" he whispers. "I thought, that night in the tub, I thought you liked me. And when I bring the eggs round in the morning. I had the feeling that you liked me then, too. But I could be wrong, you can always be wrong, so before we get wherever we're going, can't you just tell me? Because I like you like fire."

She laughs a little. Puts her hand to her windblown bob. Before she can say anything, a great white shape comes careening down the frozen meadow, down the mountains and the barrels and the house on the horizon. It lands next to her—a pelican with wings as wide as a giant's arms. It takes Zelda's fingers gently, so, so gently, in its beak. Standing between his girl and a boy who just needs to be seen so bad he'd turn on all the lights in hell.

"Mr. Puss-Boots!" she cries in delight. Mr. Puss-Boots does a little shuffling dance with his webbed feet. "Well, Frankie, I'll tell you," Zelda says cheerfully. "I do like you. I like you plenty. But I like a lot of things that are no good for me. Liking something doesn't mean much, if you ask me. It's not what matters. What matters is if you let the liking have its say. and I don't. If I can help it."

B3

PEARL DE AGOSTI Y Candela y Slake isn't hard to find. She's standing outside the great skeleton house. She's got a man's nightshirt on and stockings with holes in them. Somebody else's tie, a gold and green chevroned number, hangs around her neck and just at this moment it looks like a king's mantle draped over her shoulders. Her hair's all loose, her lipstick and eyeliner gone a-roving. She's got a cigar in one hand and a jar full of gin in the other, and she's laughing, laughing like for once that damned chicken crossed the road for something really good. Frankie only ever saw her once before. She was all slicked back, not just her hair but her heart, her clothes and her way of talking, her hand on her son's head, the way her eyes narrowed when she watched her husband cutting the ribbon for the new golfballroom. That was over now. Little Cass jumps and giggles beside her, with buttercups in his hair, and every once in awhile the little boy sings: my mummy she has blue, blue eyes! She'll forget with a wink of the left, she'll forget-you-not with a wink of the right, and if you bring me sweets she'll spend the night! in his small trembling voice. Pearl sweeps him up in her arms and covers him with kisses and calls him her prince and presses her cheek to his and Frankie doesn't know but I'll spill—it's the biggest love that boy will ever know, down there in Canada, in the dark. Funniest thing about love, how it shakes loose when no one's looking. How the dark helps it along. Maybe that's why we dug caves so much, way back when. Caspar gone for a moment and Little Cass turns into Little P, all her own, and isn't he clever, isn't he grand? He looks like himself down here, not like that pile of shit with the wedding ring on. And she just lets go into her love. Turns out she's got a bucketful. She always thought she'd gone dry.

Pearl puts her kidlet down and throws dice against the foot of the buttress. A ring of men cheer. She cheers. Her cheers sound like screaming. The dice explode against the wall into pages, pages and pages, landing on the snow like ash, covered in type, covered in good paragraphs, cutting, incisive, perfect paragraphs like her old Underwood could never bash out. She falls on them, holding them in clumps and sheafs to her heart, stuffing them in her shirt till they stick out like tits. But in a minute she's up again, into the throng of the house without walls, into the heat of the place, the sound, the fury, the utter din of it.

And Frankie sees it all, the orgy of making.

Enzo kissing out his paintings with Ollie, kissing up her columns, Murray pouring out his sculptures, Nickel and Dime dancing till blueprints for buildings that ache to look at spool out under their feet. Iris Wiltsey Charlestoning movies her man Sammy won't ever let her direct. And isn't that Lily Greer vomiting up a new Vaudeville show? Why it is, it is! Look at the magician's rabbit scrabbling up out of the toilet! And Frankie recognizes others, even if he doesn't know their real names—Cinderella dancing with Rapunzel, Jorindel breaking plates with Prince Charming, Snow White passed out cold in the front hallway while the Snow Queen holds a compress to her head. Sonnets leak out of the cloth.

And Frankie sees something else, too. He sees Vollstead,. though he doesn't know that funny muscled bow-legged goblin has a name. He sees Vollstead using that rich man's magic he himself used so well an hour ago. Following up behind, quiet as you please, the help, the janitor, the maid, picking up the dice-pages and the dance-flicks and the kiss-paintings, sweeping them up into ditches dug through the January ground, tidying everything away.

And in those ditches, the pages and the canvases and the film and the pigment and the icons and the statues liquify. Go black and bubble into syrup, into a foamy river flowing out and up and over, out and up and over into the great barrels in a thousand streams of a dark black-violet heady something that Frankie's pretty sure would fetch more money than gold in the Artemisia right about now. Zelda's hooch, bright and cold and full of dreams. He gapes like a kid, though he wants to play it cool. Zelda grins. She's proud. So proud.

"Isn't it something?" she breathes.

"You've been feeding us…junk? Upstairs. Letting us drink what you sweep up down here?"

Ollie's voice cuts through the jiggly music-palace noise. She strides up in her long trousers and suit-coat and locks arms with Zelda like they're old Greek soldiers and he's from out of town. Oleander Coy looks him up and down like he's nothing. Like she has to squint to see him at all. "Letting you? Haven't you got eyes? It's not junk, dummy, it's art! And honey, everybody eats art and drinks stories. It's the best drunk there is! If you can make something out of a potato so good that people would shoot you dead in the street for a glass, what can you make out of Enzo's pictures and Olive's dresses and my one-liners and Murray's little stone gods? Vollstead showed us how. And Al. Hell, down here I don't even have to use a white man's name. I'm me and everyone knows it. Everyone sees me."

Zelda lays her head on her friend's shoulder. Some mean little part of Frankie wonders what a flat full of girls get up to in the off-hours, and Mr. Puss-Boots nips his hip in punishment. Frankie yelps. Zelda keeps talking.

"It's…it's so direct, you know? You look at a painting and it fills you up. You read a book and sometimes it's so good you feel like you could live on it. And now we do live on it. Everyone does. It's perfect. You should try it. You're a writer. I remember!" Zelda Fair turns up her face and good lord but her lips look like glory and he stops thinking about the four of them crammed into Room 1550. "Come on. Kiss me. Let's make a book!"

Well, Frankie is in no shape to turn that down. He kisses her hard, because he knows it might be his only chance. Their tongues meet in that oh-so-natural way, the way that says they might do all right if they got married. No teeth knocking. No nose-battling. And out of their mouths and their hands come not even pages but words, just words, moving type, slick and hard and hot, words like children's toys, Christmas ornaments, crystalline creatures swelling up and flowing out of them, whispering, giggling, the words, the words that Frankie can never find, the words he reaches for and misses, and then falls back on a new detective, a new dead body, the same old yarn he's always fraying. He stops kissing Zelda because some things are more important than kisses and the poor kid lurches after the black, dancing words, trying to hold onto them, trying to stop them getting away, trying to read them so he can remember, so he can remember when all this is over how good he can be, how simple and clean and orderly and beautiful. And not for a minute does he think that he only kissed those words into the world because Zelda put her mouth on his, that they're hers, too. Not for a heartbeat.

The words don't care. They leap toward the ditches, dive into the liquor, shiver into the brew and the barrels. Frankie sobs after them. He hates this place. This place where he isn't seen right, where he was only allowed once everyone else had already gone. It's not a Minnesota kind of place. His words are lost and he can never love a place that showed him what he could do and then took it away. Everyone here is out to lunch, bonkers, mad—Zelda is shooting a tommy gun at the sky and stories are falling back down into her hair. She's catching them in a cut-glass pitcher, laughing, running to snatch another from the air, and sometimes she grabs their crystal words, too, their hard dark typeface animals Frankie and Zelda made together, skittering and tripping on the ice. They all fizz into rum in her pitcher, a deep green rum shining with wonderful light.

Frankie doesn't care. He had it. He had it, there in his hands, the book he's meant to write, all the books, the books deep down in the bottom of him, the pure sentences and chapters that get so damn junked up on the way out. And they're gone, turned to muck so idiots can guzzle them down and puke them up and hallucinate on the fire escape and then forget it all in the morning. They're a ruin, they are ruin, and he can never get them back. So Frankie does what a young man does when he's lost something he thinks he's got a right to, when he's going to be seen, by god, when he's stuck on the other side of the shop window while all the other kids roll around in the candy canes. Frankie Key snatches Zelda's gun away. She yelps like he didn't when the lady in the ballroom lost her shoe in his back pocket.

He grabs Pearl by the arm. She just laughs because who knows what a bastard grabbing you at a party will make here? A trumpet solo soars out of her elbow, golden notes and clefs bursting like sweet artillery, the melody loud and clear as rain.

"You're coming home," Frankie snarls. "You're coming with me. Your husband sent me. Put your clothes on."

"Fuck you," Pearl giggles, and Little Cass pipes up, repeating his mother. "Fuckoo!"

"Hey now," gruffs a voice, which is Vollstead's voice. Frankie looks him dead in the eye. "Stop that monkey shit. We can settle this like men, yeah?" Frankie stares. Takes in V's machine-gun legs, his ripply blue chest, his warty odd face and his long ears, his earrings, his gold eyes, his huge hands, and our boy up and decides Vollstead isn't real, he just isn't. He's like the space between the restaurants in the lobby, the paisley green-and-gold place where you whisper about gruyere and boysenberries but it isn't really anything at all, just a whispering place like St. Paul's in London. This ugly lump is just one of Al's tricks. Al loves tricks. They're his favorites. And Frankie's going to take Pearl home and get paid enough to buy his own place to sit and think and try to remember those pristine words he lost. No abracadabra is going to get in the way of that, no sir. No bunny is gonna show him up. Not this bunny, anyway, this fairybook monster with breath like sweet almonds and the death of hope.

So Frankie shoots him.

B4

PARTIES GET QUIET TOWARD the end. Only a few folks left, keeping the lights on, keeping the music going, rooting through the bottles for the one that's not empty. Gets quiet. Just before the sun starts straightening the tables and filling the glasses. Gets close and secret and gentle. Truth o'clock. That's where we are now.

Al doesn't care about punishment in the traditional sense. Eye for an eye and all that. Al can have an eye whenever he wants. An eye's nothing to him. He'd rather have an eyelash for an eye. Or the USS Maine for an eye. He has no sense of proportion, does Al. But he has a mean sense of humor. Vollstead was his baby. A wedding ring he traded back and forth with his great big Titanic-Titania dinosaur-wife. Zelda's his baby, too. And Pearl. And Ollie. And Enzo. They're all his babies. He could kill Frankie and nobody would even get upset over it. Fair play, old man. A dozen more where he came from. But it's not even that much fun to kill humans. Al got bored with that centuries ago. He needs his fun. No cat likes to be fed dazed mice. You gotta play with them a little first, or the meat gets tough.

So here they sit, in the close quiet dark of the grand party. Around a table: Al, Frankie, Zelda, Ollie, Pearl with Little Cass in her lap. The table's the same green as the Golfballroom in the Artemisia, soft and fake and nice. Al deals cards like an old pro because that's just what he is. A plain red Bicycle deck, nothing fancy, nothing hidden, fifty-two cards fair and square, I wouldn't try to cheat you, no sir. Check 'em if you like. Four aces, nothing up the sleeve.

Zelda's fur coat hangs open just enough for everyone to see she hasn't got a stitch on underneath except a little emerald pendant on a gold chain. Green as a dock light between her breasts. Mr. Puss-Boots sleeps under her feet, his long white wings swallowing up her toes. Mr. Puss-Boots dreams a story like this, a story where a prince goes creeping down into the underworld after twelve dancing princesses because some king decided the girls were having too much fun and wanted to rub their faces in how hard he owns them. Only when Mr. Puss-Boots dreams it, the prince is half-pelican, and he loves the princesses like the sea. He just glides on down after them, into the dark, following their starry-light dresses, and when he finds them they laugh and shout and speak Pelican and hold him in their arms all together and the bird-prince just never goes back home to that nasty old daddy with the tinfoil hat. Mr. Puss-Boots stays with his girls forever and the dancing princesses never slow down. It's a nice dream. He's dreamed it every night since his first sleep in Canada.

Pearl strokes her kid's hair. Ollie smokes and plays footsie with Al. Frankie glares at the lump that used to be Vollstead. The bloody, unreal lump. Even without him, pages and paint trickle into the river flowing up to the barrels. His pages. His perfect ink.

"The game is Cretaceous Hold 'Em. Everything's wild. Play or I bury you here." Al doesn't fuck around. But his voice is so soft and loving, like a grandpa after a good pipe. Only grandpa might eat you as soon as tuck you in bed.

The cards fan out but nobody wants to bet. No chips anyhow. Zelda looks at her cards. Three queens. She touches their faces. Olive's face and Ollie's face and Opal's face. Spades, Hearts, Clubs. Red Bicycle my ass, she thinks. She puts her hand into her coat. Her comforting coat. All she wants is to shoot up another chapter, is to dance some wry, wise prose into the bathroom floor. It is so good here, she thinks. It is hers. There is no space between wanting and having, between thinking and making real. That's the best any place can offer. She does have something to bet, she thinks, though she was saving it. What if she needed it? Well, she guesses she needs it now. Zelda Fair puts her syringe in the middle of the table. Al looks approvingly at her.

"My girl," he says.

Pearl takes off her ruby earrings and throws them in. Little Cass tries to add his lollipop but his mama won't let him waste his treasure. Ollie puts in her smokes. Frankie? Frankie has fuck all, to tell the truth. He throws in his billfold, which is hardly enough to call, let alone stay in the game. Honestly, Frankie. Get with it. Al pulls off his cufflink. He says:

"It's not a cufflink. It's Lily Greer. She's gonna shoot somebody cold in the 10th floor hallway in about six months. Who's it gonna be?"

Pearl's face pinches. She knows what she's got. She calls. As she lays down her cards, Al names them:

"The lady has it all! Well done! The House has a stock market crash in two years and a hotel stripped for copper during the war and split into slum-happy squats. That, combined with your nasty round of bronchitis and jolly heroin habit around age 50, unsuccessful novel, and a dead husband on 10 gives you a flush. Congrats, Miss P, you win the pot."

Everyone recoils.

"Come on, kittens!" Al crows. "The cards are king! What's Wall Street but fairy gold anyway? Don't worry! I've had that shindig planned for a dog's age. But Pearly's got a 2 and a 9 of diamonds—that sets the clock. 1929! Isn't this a good game? Poker is my best invention."

Pearl smiles. She smiles like Christmas and Little Cass clings to her. She wraps her long fingers around the syringe like Lily Greer's gun and puts it in her arm to keep it safe, jams it in before anyone can stop her. She'll take it all if Big Cass gets his. That's fine. Fine as a Yale crew team rowing in the sun.

The cards come out again. Whick, whick, whick.

Zelda looks at Frankie. He looks like her Daddy. He looks like a book she hasn't thought up yet. He looks like a bear on a chain growling I love you. She's so drunk she can't think. Drunk on her own supply, on her insides turned outside and boiled into a glass. She takes off her green necklace. Al gave it to her. Gave it to her when she sold her first case of the good stuff. He kissed her when he did it. It was like kissing Neptune. The planet, not the sailor-man. The whole planet, too. The storm on its equator and all the moons. Frankie pulls out his skeleton key, the magic stick that lets him into any room and good thing he's a pretty honest fella or it might be a worry that he's got one. Pearl tosses in her other earring. Small change. She's done, she's happy, she's not fussed about anything else. Al pulls out his other cufflink.

"It's not a cufflink," he says. "It's a name. A name that goes forever, a name schoolkids read about in a hundred years and say wow, that so-and-so was a hell of a writer. Maybe if I hope and pray and huff and puff I'll be that good, huh? Who wants it?"

This time there's betting. You better believe it. Pearl's not so la-dee-da now. She gets her cards and puts in her tie, her stockings, finally her shirt. Ollie keeps her cool but only barely. She puts in her notebook, her blue pen, the name she uses in the big bad city so no one sees her straight. Frankie antes a safety pin, a cherry candy, and at last, as sullen as icemelt in March, his own notepad and pen. Ollie rolls her eyes.

"How original," she quips.

Al's happy to raise. A hip flask, a cigarette case (full), and last, a strand of his own hair.

"It's not a flask. It's a life in Paris. And these ain't cigarettes, they're a sanatorium upstate—a nice one, I promise! Hydrotherapy, electro-convulsive, thorazine, the whole smorgasbord. No expense spared. But this really is my hair. Honest Thomas. Just a hair. But this hair turns into a marriage when you take it upstairs. A long one. Long is all I can do. Can't do happy, can't do easy, can't do pretty. But heaven and the dodo knows I can do long."

Zelda only has two things left. Two things she's willing to wager. She puts in her matchstick first. The blue head looks awful to her. She shivers. Al names his own bets, but they don't name theirs. But Miss Z knows his games by now, at least a few, and she's pretty sure her syringe and Pearl's earrings and Ollie's everything and Frankie's ridiculous safety pin have other names, too. The matchstick is so red. Wasn't it blue a second ago?

Without even meaning to, without even knowing why, she whispers: "It's not a matchstick. It's death by fire. Locked in a room and nobody coming for you." Nobody says a thing. What can you say? Zelda's sure she's gonna win. She started all this. She didn't shoot anybody. It's hers.

But that's not enough to stay in. So Zelda slips out of her black fur coat, a snail sliding out of a shell, bright and bare and just horribly, viciously vulnerable. You almost want to squash it just for daring to come out. Silly thing. What's it thinking?

Oleander Coy opens up her arm and bleeds onto the table. All in. Frankie's cherry candy, Pearl's baby boy. Zelda starts crying. She only has the one thing left. She doesn't want to put it in the pot. It's hers. She loves it. She can't get it back if she loses it. And suddenly that win-feel goes up like gas. Zelda knows, somehow, that it's all over now, all over down here, with Vollstead dead. Something's unhappy in Canada and Al's gonna pack up shop. This is the end of the party. It's truth o'clock. But she doesn't want to go home. She doesn't want to go back. Going back is the worst thing she can think of. Being who she was. Marrying Billy or Josie or…God, she can't even remember the other one's name. She's still young enough to think she's just driving down one long road forward and up, never looping back. It's mine, it's mine, she cries, but it's this or lose, and losing a game with Al is like losing one with gravity.

Zelda Fair puts a bottle on the table. It's square, like Bombay Sapphire. Hell, maybe it was a Bombay Sapphire bottle in another life. The label's all rubbed off now. It's full of green, the green of her last shots, her last pages—and some of her last kisses, too, but mostly the divine fire-paper bullets of the gun Vollstead gave her, the green rum of her heart, her best heart, her heart beaten out into a long, lovely tale where a girl comes out on top and the beats come so hot and hard and sweet they'll knock you dead and you'll beg for a sequel.

All in. She's got nothing left.

Pearl's out right quick. Nothing but rubbish and she doesn't care. Little Cass chews on her Jack and Al doesn't say it but that

Jack is a suicide at thirty-five. Poor lamb. Ollie puts down eights over twos. She's shaking, her pretty ink-stained mouth trembling. Still bleeding. Zelda puts pressure on the wound with one hand and lays her cards out with the other. Not as good as her three queens. Just a pair of sevens.

But Frankie? Frankie has a full house.

Al doesn't even show his cards. Just counts out the boy's winnings.

"Good show, you little milquetoast fuckhearted sludge," he chuckles. He'd never admit it, but he played fair. Just let them roll. That's what you get when sit down with fairies. The House doesn't ever hurt. Fair odds are as good as damnation. "The House has cirrhosis of the liver and a healthy baby daughter, to which you add fourteen novels, a decade spent as the toast of the town, and an early, penniless death! It's all yours, son. The nights in Paris, the long marriage, the asylum with the beautiful gardens, just the right size for a wife who's no fun anymore, the forever-name, the liver, the out-of-print back catalogue, the ding-dong-dead, the lot! I've played some sharks in my time, but you've bested me. Not many can put that on their resume. Aren't you proud? Couldn't you just crow? Couldn't you just howl?"

Al's face goes dark and small.

"Now get the fuck out of my house."

ROOFTOP

ZELDA DOESN'T WANT TO go. She wants the brandy-sun of Canada and Al's Neptune kisses and her gun. She wants Ollie and Mr. Puss-Boots. What did she do wrong? She loved Vollstead. Why should she have to go? She doesn't even remember the name of the hotel. When it's above ground, it has a different name. Right? She thinks so. She's sure of it.

Between you and me, I think Al would've let her stay. If she begged. He likes monkeys begging. Never gets tired of that song. Ollie stayed. A few others. Ask Persephone. All you gotta do is open up a tab at the bar. Who wants to go back to being unseen and unseeable? Besides, hell has the best theater.

But Zelda didn't even ask. Why?

Because Frankie has her stash.

There was a moment there when people just keeled over faint for what Zelda had. Not her face, not her hand, not to get between her legs. But for her Goodies. For her Good. And she won't ever be able to live without that now. Without rum and love and Good. Frankie's got the last of it. He thinks he's smuggled it without her seeing. He can feel it warming him up already. Zelda followed him up that long staircase, through the door in her own room—seems like forever ago she tried to have Harold bust it open. As if you could break into a place that always wanted you. She follows him and he's better than Orpheus I guess. He never once looks back to see if she's there.

They come out onto the roof in time for him to start collecting eggs for the morning delivery.

"Hey there, Dido," he calls to the five hundred white chickens all together, all one name, all one queen. "Time to give it up."

The sun, the real sun, is starting to peek up over the rooftops of New York. The goats mew and moan, full of milk and attitude, chewing the real ballroom grass growing up on top of the Artemisia, her green, green hair, her crown of living things. The bees yawn noisily. The Jersey cows snuff their wet noses at the puffs of light. Rutherford roars softly, if a fella can roar softly, and Zelda'll be damned if it doesn't sound like I love you after all.

Frankie stops for a second. Thinks hard. Zelda knows what boys look like when they think hard. He looks around like Josie did before he proposed for the first time. He turns to her and takes her hand in his. His pockets are so stuffed with his winnings he looks like a horse with saddlebags. He says he loves her—sure. He says Al gave them a life together—sure, fine. Let's take it and run. Whatever you say, just give it back, Zelda begs silently. Just give it back and we'll do it all. Paris, the kid, the books, the everything. Everything in me and you and five hundred chickens and a talking bear on top.

"If we're gonna get married, we gotta share everything," he says softly. She doesn't want to, but she sure as hell wants to share.

Frankie Key gives it back.

Zelda lunges for it, for her own darling green-bright heart—but it's not her rum Frankie's handing over. It's her matchstick. Her death by fire. He thinks he's being kind. Generous. He puts her coat around her shoulders, her black fur like her own skin. Sure, fine. Matchstick, coat. Third time's a charm. Give it back, give it back.

He offers her a cigarette from Al's silver case. And that's all.

Zelda wonders if he knows that she'll follow him anywhere for it. All the rest of her days. That he'll lose her if she puts her hands on it, like a selkie skin. She'll take it and run. Run forever.

"It's mine," she whispers. "It's the best part of me and you took it."

"I won it."

"It's not yours."

Frankie won't meet her eyes. "We'll share it," he says. Zelda breathes a little. Better than nothing. Better than empty.

Frankie Key tends to the five hundred Didos. The five hundred eggs on top of the world. He holds the bottle tight in his trousers, hiding it from her with his turned back. He will drink it all and he will remember and he will write it all. Write something big. Zelda will understand. She owes him. She let him see what he could make and then took it away. It's only right. It's restitution. She will forgive him by Paris. She will read it and see how good he is and know how it had to be. He'll make it up to her.

Don't do it, boy. You can't make up this kind of thing.

But he won't listen. Up there on top of the Artemisia, in the dawn like shots firing madly, fire in the barrel and holes opening in the dark, secret and furtive behind the bear's belly, Frankie Key sucks down the rumglory of the underworld, the hurtling life of the hotel stuck like a pin all the way through the world, Zelda's pin, her bullets, her Goodies, her.

The light glitters off the bottle like sequins on a green, green dress.

CHECK-OUT

NOT MUCH LEFT, KITTENS. Just you and me and the rest of the miserable bastards left over at the end of this story.

Who am I?

Well. I told you it wasn't a good book. I have such trouble with that trick of cutting up what really happens and stitching it together with what didn't or couldn't or shouldn't happen. I just can't help telling you what happened, in the order it happened. No art to it. I could have made myself nicer, a better mother, a saint with a soul of marzipan. But it seemed like too much work. Maybe you've heard it told different by somebody you liked better and believed it—that's fine by me. I just told you what I know. The inside of a hotel the size of the world. On the outside, I suppose it just looked like a bunch of assholes drinking themselves stupid and putting on airs.

Now when I threw the dice in a man's tie? That was better. That was what I wanted to say. But you try telling everybody your dream five years after you dreamt it, and with a nasty cough, too.

I guess I only know one more thing, my little ducks. Then it's good night and good riddance and every other good thing and bus your own tables if you know what's good for you. You don't have to go home but you can't stay here. That old rag.

Frankie and Zelda lit out pretty soon after that morning on the rooftop. She stayed long enough to tell me about it. I made her tea. You talk to the people who've hurt like you've hurt, and there weren't so many of us at that table. Nobody ever asked those dancing princesses how they liked life once that fella kicked them out of the magic downtown club where they could be infinite together. I bet they didn't care for it. I bet they talked about it, even ninety years on, twelve old queens who can buy their own damn shoes. I bet they made each other tea. It's the least you can do.

So Zelda sat and sipped told me she helped take the eggs down that morning. She liked it. It was methodical. Basket, door, basket, door. And she said that once or twice, just once or twice, before she knocked on a door in her fur with nothing underneath, she thought one of the eggs shook itself. Like a dog trying to get the water off its back. It shook and stretched and turned every color all at once—and then nothing, white as cake again.

She told me that like it might worry me. But I told you about Al and his people. How rarely they nest. How rarely they make any more of themselves. And I figure a nest, for a fella like Al, isn't some little mess of twigs up in a tree. It's gotta be big. It's gotta be grand. It's gotta go all the way up to the clouds and all the way down to hell.

I figure it might look like a hotel.